# THE BARON'S RETURN

## LANDING A LORD

## SUZANNA MEDEIROS

Copyright © 2023 by Saozinha Medeiros

The Baron's Return
First Digital Edition: April 2023
First Print Edition: April 2023
Cover design © Kim Killion
Edited by Victory Editing
ebook ISBN: 978-1-988223-39-1
Paperback ISBN: 978-1-988223-40-7

This is a work of fiction. Names, characters, places, and incidents either are the product of the author's imagination or are used fictitiously, and any resemblance to actual persons, living or dead, business establishments, events, or locales is entirely coincidental.

All rights reserved. Except as permitted under the U.S. Copyright Act of 1976, no part of this publication may be reproduced, stored in or introduced into a retrieval system, or transmitted, in any form, or by any means (electronic, mechanical, photocopying, recording, or otherwise), without the prior written permission of the author.

# THE BARON'S RETURN

*She broke his heart once before. He won't give her the chance
to do it again.*

Baron Cranston doesn't believe in happily-ever-
afters. Experience has taught him that love is a risk
not worth taking.

Forced to marry another man when she was
younger, Abigail didn't know she was carrying
Cranston's child until after he'd entered military
service. Now widowed and out of mourning, she is
no longer trapped in a union she never wanted.

When Abigail tells Cranston about his daughter, she
doesn't expect his proposal. But their marriage of

convenience could give her the second chance she never dreamed possible. Now she only needs to convince the cynical baron that his heart isn't as closed off as he believes.

To learn about Suzanna Medeiros's future books, you can sign up for her newsletter at https://www. suzannamedeiros.com/newsletter.

# CHAPTER 1

*London, July 1817*

It was the perfect day for a wedding. The temperature was warm but not unbearable, and the clouds had parted for the happy couple. Baron Cranston was surrounded by smiling, happy faces, but the only thing on his mind was how he'd rather be anywhere else.

He'd learned many years ago that love was a fantasy people told themselves existed so they could get through the daily monotony of life. Some of the people who went searching for their happily-ever-afters were lucky enough to find companions who held similar foolish notions. They were the fortunate ones.

Then there was the rest of the world. People who were content merely to find a partner who wasn't intolerable, whom they could show off as a status symbol, or whom could provide them with a comfortable life. But for people like him, who'd thought they found love and who'd had their dreams of matrimonial bliss crushed, they recognized love was an illusion.

Cranston would never again give a woman the power to break his heart. Even if he wanted to try, a part of him would always be wary. Always be waiting for the inevitable betrayal that would come.

Still, he couldn't deny the pang of envy that went through him as he watched Viscount Ashford repeat his vows. Not that Cranston would ever admit it.

Brushing off the unwelcome emotion as a lingering remnant of crushed dreams, he managed a hearty congratulations to his friend and his new bride as they gathered outside the wedding chapel that warm morning.

The Marquess of Lowenbrock clapped him on the shoulder. "You're welcome to ride back to the house with us for the wedding breakfast."

The three of them—Cranston, Ashford, and Lowenbrock—had formed a tight bond during their years of military service. Their friendship was as strong as ever now that they had given up their commission and returned to England last year. But as the only one still unmarried, Cranston was very aware of being the odd man out.

Cranston shook his head. "I brought my carriage and will see you there shortly."

Lowenbrock merely nodded and headed toward his own carriage. The one that held his wife of less than one year and whom Cranston had recently learned was carrying their first child.

He rolled his shoulders to ease the tension that was starting to build at the base of his neck. Normally he did a better job of hiding his feelings, but there was no denying that weddings would always bring up bad memories for him.

Lowenbrock and Ashford knew he didn't believe in love and happily-ever-afters. Not for himself. But he had no doubt that his friends would defy the odds and remain blissfully wed.

He was about to head to his own carriage when he noticed the intense discussion taking place between the new bride and groom. He'd expected the pair to be gazing at one another with adoration, but instead, they stood off to one side, deep in conversation.

Ashford shook his head, and Cranston watched as Mary placed a hand on his arm. Then Ashford turned to meet his gaze and Cranston knew. They were talking about him.

He started for his carriage, trying to push back the unease that had only increased with that significant look. He stopped when Ashford called out to him.

Somehow he managed a casual tone. "Shouldn't you be whisking your wife away? Taking advantage of a few stolen moments in the carriage before you must greet your guests at the wedding breakfast?"

When Ashford's expression remained grim, Cranston could feel the hairs stand up along his arms. He'd always had the same feeling just before a battle when they were still in the military. He squared his shoulders and braced himself for what was coming.

"Before we return to the house, I need to warn you. Mary invited Lady Holbrook."

Cranston felt those words like a blow to the stomach. Not only would he be forced to watch his two closest friends enjoy themselves with their wives, but now he would have his greatest mistake thrown into his face at the same time.

Abigail was going to be there.

He'd caught sight of her the month before at Hyde Park. After that day, he'd avoided the park during the fashionable hour. But it seemed he hadn't been successful in avoiding this inevitable meeting.

Cranston nodded. "Thank you for telling me."

Ashford shook his head. "One of the things I love most about my wife is her practical nature, but I've discovered that she has a strong romantic streak. She told me that she likes the woman, but I fear she might be matchmaking. Hoping that you'll find someone and join us in wedded bliss."

Cranston couldn't hold back his bark of laughter. The way his friend's mouth twisted as he said the words made it clear that he knew it was a ridiculous statement. When Cranston did finally choose a bride, it wouldn't be for love. And it definitely wouldn't be Abigail Holbrook.

Ashford winced. "I know. I told her to leave the matter alone, but she went ahead and issued the invitation without telling me."

"You told her." That realization shouldn't have felt like a betrayal.

"She saw the way you looked at the woman that day in Hyde Park. When she told me that she hoped to befriend Lady Holbrook, I had to explain why that wouldn't be a good idea."

Cranston wasn't angry with his friend. He'd been in love once, and he had no doubt the man he'd been back then would have done the same thing. He liked Ashford's new wife. She wasn't flighty and seemed to have a good head on her shoulders. And she did care about others, almost too much it seemed. Still, it bothered him that Ashford and his new wife had discussed him. And despite that, the new viscountess was still trying to push him toward the woman who'd broken his heart.

"If anyone asks, I can tell them you had some-where else to be. We'll be in London for the rest of the day and can see you later."

Cranston shook his head. He'd run from the woman once already. Her betrayal had been the reason he'd chosen to buy a commission nine years ago. He was done running. Still, he couldn't help but wonder if Abigail knew he was good friends with Ashford and, by extension, the man's wife. The cynical side of him refused to believe that their upcoming meeting was coincidental.

"Nothing and no one will keep me away."

Ashford nodded and turned to rejoin his wife.

Wife. If things had gone as planned all those years ago, Cranston would have been the first of his friends to wed. Although if that had happened, he wouldn't have met Ashford or Lowenbrock. They would likely only be acquaintances now.

His emotions were in turmoil as he strode to his carriage. But by the time he arrived at Ashford's town house, he'd have them in check again.

One corner of his mouth rose as he contemplated the meeting ahead. Perhaps it was time for him to go on the attack. If his time in military service had taught him anything, it was that one was already doomed if they feared losing before stepping onto the battlefield. No, if Abigail was going to be joining him in this battle, it was he who would come out the victor.

# CHAPTER 2

It didn't take Abigail long to realize she'd made a mistake in accepting the invitation to Miss Mary Trenton and the Viscount Ashford's wedding breakfast. But not because Gideon was here. She'd known he was a good friend of the groom and had assumed he'd be in attendance.

No matter when it happened, their first meeting was going to be awkward. But a small, no doubt masochistic, part of her had dreamed that he would take one look at her and realize he still loved her.

No, coming here today was a mistake because Gideon, who was now Baron Cranston, clearly wasn't experiencing the same regret and tumult of emotion at being in the same room again after so many years apart. In fact, he scarcely noticed her.

After congratulating the newly married couple and offering them her wishes for a happy future, she'd proceeded to the drawing room where a number of guests had gathered. She knew a few of the people here but not well. She greeted a few of them as she passed, wary of running into Gideon.

She knew exactly when he arrived. It had always been like this with Gideon. He had only to walk into a room and her body seemed to vibrate with awareness at his presence. She turned to look at the doorway and waited for him to notice her.

He scanned the room, taking in all the guests. Abigail didn't miss the way the women near him whispered, but her attention was only on him. Her breath caught when his eyes finally landed on her. She wasn't sure what she'd expected, but it certainly hadn't been indifference. His gaze continued his sweep of the room. He gave no indication that he'd even recognized her, and the snub felt like a physical blow.

When he strode toward his friend and the new Viscountess Ashford, he dropped a kiss on the woman's hand and winked at her. She couldn't deny the warmth in his expression, evident even from where she stood, as he smiled at the viscountess. A hint of jealousy sparked within her.

Which was ridiculous. From all accounts, Gideon and the viscount were good friends, so of course he would know the man's bride. Abigail's jealousy wasn't logical, but then feelings rarely were. She'd pinned so much hope on this first meeting with him and couldn't deny that his rejection of everything they'd once shared caused a hurt that threatened to steal her breath.

Which she supposed was only fair. Hadn't she done the same to him all those years ago? She'd rejected him with a cruelty that was aimed at ensuring he stopped pursuing her.

She turned away from the sight of him chatting amiably with the other woman, wanting nothing more than to flee the house. She couldn't put off their meeting forever, but it didn't need to happen in the company of so many people.

"Lady Holbrook, it is so good to see you here." Lady Lowenbrock smiled warmly as she came to a stop next to her.

"I wouldn't have missed this joyous occasion," Abigail said by way of greeting, grateful for the distraction. She'd met both the marchioness and the new Lady Ashford the month before. Lady Lowenbrock was married to another of Gideon's good friends. "But please call me Abigail. I don't like to stand on formality with friends."

The marchioness inclined her head. "Of course. And you should call me Amelia." She lowered her voice. "Can you follow me out into the hallway?"

She nodded in reply, wondering what the woman wanted to say to her that couldn't be said in this room. As she followed Amelia from the drawing room, she imagined that she could feel Gideon's eyes on her. But she resisted the temptation to look at him. She didn't need yet another disappointment if he was still ignoring her.

They walked past a group of people who were gathered just outside the drawing room and moved farther down the hallway. Finally the marchioness came to a stop when there was no danger they'd be overheard.

"Is something the matter?" Abigail kept her voice low, but it didn't seem that anyone was paying them the slightest attention.

Amelia's mouth twisted in a small grimace. "I apologize for the dramatics. I just needed to speak to you and wanted to do so in private to save you any embarrassment."

A frisson of alarm snaked down her spine, and

she suspected the worst. Gideon had asked this woman to tell her that her presence wasn't welcome here. She took a deep breath. "I understand. I'll just say my goodbyes to Lord and Lady Ashford, and then I'll go."

Abigail started to turn, but Amelia placed a hand on her arm to stop her. "Oh no, you misunderstand me. I'm not asking you to leave."

Well, now she felt positively ridiculous. Of course Gideon wouldn't have gone to the trouble of having her barred from the house. Not when it was clear she held no significance in his life.

"I'm sorry if I alarmed you," Amelia said. "I just wanted to warn you that Mary is playing matchmaker. She's hoping to make a match between you and Lord Cranston."

Abigail's stomach dipped. She had to swallow hard before she could speak. "What do you know?"

Amelia sighed. "Nothing, but I got the distinct impression something more was going on. I saw the way you watched him when he arrived. And I saw that his eyes passed over you completely. I thought…" She raised one shoulder. "I'm not sure what I thought. I fear I've misspoken. I know that Lord Cranston is very popular with the fairer sex. If you've asked Mary for an introduction, please ignore my misplaced warning. I've been told I have something of an overactive imagination."

Abigail let out a small laugh. This woman was far too astute. She only hoped that no one else thought she was pining after the man. "No, you are correct. Gid—Lord Cranston and I knew each other once, many years ago. But it would seem he has no wish to renew the acquaintance." She shook her head. "Perhaps it is better that I leave. I knew he'd be here and never should have come."

"Nonsense," Amelia said. "I will remain by your side until it is time to eat. If you no longer require my presence, you can just tell me that you see my husband looking for me."

Abigail was amazed at this woman's generosity when they were little more than acquaintances. "Why would you help me? I would have thought your loyalties would lie with your husband's friends."

Amelia tilted her head to one side. "Why must there be sides? He hasn't asked me to choose, and I assume you're not asking that of me either. But I won't force you to stay if you wish to take your leave."

Abigail couldn't deny that she didn't want to flee. Not when there was still a chance she'd be able to speak to Gideon again. His casual indifference to her presence had been a blow, but she would regret it more if she ran away now. Given the way they'd parted, she'd been a fool to think he would want to speak to her again. But that only meant she would have to try harder. There was too much at stake to give up now.

"I'd like to stay."

"Then the matter is settled. Mary likes you a great deal, and since I've always known her to be the best judge of character, I'm sure we'll soon become friends."

Amelia threaded her arm through Abigail's, and they made their way to the drawing room.

"Have you met Lord Ashford's family?" Amelia asked, her voice a little too loud as they reentered the room. "Oh, I see his sister, Lady Benington, right there."

# CHAPTER 3

It was almost impossible to ignore Abigail's presence, but Cranston did everything in his power to appear unaffected by her. He was careful to hide how he kept her in his periphery and tracked her movements. He would never again allow the woman to gain the upper hand.

Abigail had grown more beautiful over the years, and he hated that he wasn't immune to her. He'd allowed himself to believe that when they met again, he'd feel only indifference for her. Instead, he couldn't deny that he still wanted her.

He hadn't expected the desire that threatened to undo his reserve when his eyes swept over her. A desire that refused to go away no matter whom he flirted with, and heaven knew there were a number of attractive women here. He'd been with a few of them, but none held Abigail's appeal. Which meant that he must possess a previously undetected streak of masochism.

He was speaking to Lowenbrock when he saw the man's wife step out of the room with Abigail. He barely held back a curse. How was it possible that his two closest friends were married to women who seemed intent on befriending the one woman in all of England he wanted to avoid?

When it was time to sit down for the wedding breakfast, he half expected to find that Ashford's new wife had seated Abigail next to him. Fortunately he was spared that ordeal. Perhaps she'd taken Ashford's warning about meddling in the affairs of others to heart after all.

At least he'd be free from Mary's well-meaning interference soon. Ashford and his bride were leaving for Brighton tomorrow on their wedding trip. After that, they planned to return to Ashford's country seat in Suffolk. They wouldn't be in London again until Parliament was in session next year.

For the sake of propriety, he offered Abigail a polite nod as he passed her to take his seat. He wanted to ignore her altogether, but others would notice. He wouldn't ruin Ashford's wedding day by doing anything to cause a scandal.

Footmen set out platters of breakfast food along the center of the table. Many of the women gravitated straight to the cakes and other sweets. Cranston intended to enjoy them as well, but first he'd have his fill of the hot rolls, ham, and eggs. It appeared that most of the other men present were also starting with the heartier fare.

He had to grit his teeth when he heard the sound of Abigail's laughter. It seemed a cruel twist of fate that he could still pick out the sound in a crowded room after all these years.

He might not be sitting next to the woman who had broken his heart, but she sat close enough that it was impossible to ignore her presence. She was speaking to Mary and Amelia with great animation.

He turned to the woman on his left. Ashford's sister, Lady Benington. He kept his dalliances to widows or mature, unattached women who wouldn't expect marriage, but that didn't mean he was above flirting with a married woman.

Lord Benington slung an arm around his wife's shoulders, and Cranston barely held back a smirk at the man's not-too-subtle reminder that the woman with whom he was attempting to distract himself was already married. He needn't have bothered. Cranston had never knowingly slept with a married woman.

Lord Benington met his gaze. "Do you have any plans to return to the country? We'll be departing soon ourselves."

No doubt the same could be said for most of the people here, many of whom were still in town because they wanted to wish Ashford well. London would be emptying out soon.

"I have no immediate plans," he said before taking a healthy swallow of coffee.

Most of the guests were drinking either tea or chocolate, but he'd developed a taste for coffee during his time at war, as had Ashford and Lowen-brock. He knew the marquess would be staying in London for a few weeks. But before the summer was over, he'd be heading north to Yorkshire.

Lord Benington continued. "And you, Lady Holbrook? Will you be remaining in London?"

He stiffened at the question and turned to look at her. He couldn't help but wonder why the man would single out Abigail.

She met his gaze before looking away quickly and bestowing a smile on Lord Benington. "I've taken up residence here in London. I have no plans to return to the country."

"That makes sense," Mary said with a nod. "Now that you're out of mourning, I imagine you'd like to get out and about again. I regret that we won't be able to spend time together until Ashford and I return to town next year."

The man seated to Abigail's left asked her about her daughter, and Abigail turned to answer the question. Her voice was low, however, and Cranston couldn't make out her words.

He'd gone out of his way to avoid any news of the Dowager Viscountess Holbrook. He hadn't even wanted to think about her since resigning his commission and returning to England last year. He'd seen the new viscount, her husband's heir, during sessions in the House of Lords, but he hadn't spoken to the man.

The young, very handsome viscount whom he believed was close in age to Cranston's own thirty years. He wondered if the viscount was also staying in London and hated the spark of jealousy that flared to life within him.

Lady Benington spoke low enough that only he and her husband could hear. "Lady Holbrook is a very lovely woman, and she seems quite pleasant.

I'm happy to hear she's now out of mourning and able to… *socialize*."

His gaze shot to Ashford's sister. For a moment he feared that she, too, was a part of whatever scheme his friends' wives were planning.

He couldn't be certain, but if he had to guess, he'd say that her statement was innocent. Brought on, no doubt, by the way he'd been trying to over-hear Abigail's conversation.

Damn. At some point he'd stopped being discreet.

He smirked at the woman. "Are you inquiring about my nocturnal habits?"

Lady Benington colored, and her husband laughed at the way Cranston had put an end to her questions about Abigail. Lord Benington turned the subject to tamer ones, and Cranston spent the rest of the meal being careful not to get caught staring at Abigail again.

But that didn't mean he wasn't observing her out of the corner of his eye. She kept glancing in his direction, as she'd been doing since his arrival.

He knew exactly what that meant. She was working up the courage to approach him.

Well, he wasn't going to give her the satisfaction of catching him off guard. If there was one thing his years in the army had taught him, it was that it was always best to control the battle.

After the meal was over, he made it a point to speak to the other guests present so she wouldn't have an opportunity to approach him. When it was clear that she'd given up hope of speaking to him that morning, he went on the offensive.

She was chatting with Lowenbrock's wife when he approached.

"You've been dying to speak to me since I arrived."

Her entire body stiffened.

Amelia excused herself and left the two of them alone.

# CHAPTER 4

"Now is your chance to speak to me. You might not have another."

Abigail froze as waves of shock rolled through her body. She'd seen Amelia's eyes dart over her shoulder to watch someone approach. She'd been about to turn to see who it was but hadn't expected it to be Gideon.

Given how he'd been avoiding her, she'd been considering when and where she could find another, less public space to speak to him. She'd even considered asking the marchioness to help her in arranging a meeting somewhere where she wouldn't have to worry about others who were competing for his attention.

From the cool, clipped tones of his voice, it was

obvious he didn't want to speak to her. No doubt he saw her as someone he was forced to acknowledge, and that fact didn't give him any pleasure. It was so different from how he'd behaved with everyone else that morning, in particular the women. It didn't matter whether they were wed or not, his attention toward each had been warm and attentive. But now the edge of ice in his voice was unmistakable.

She took a deep breath and turned to face him.

He stood stock-still as he looked down at her. She wasn't blind. She'd been aware that somehow he was more handsome now than he'd been all those years ago. But it was another matter to have him standing this close to her.

He stood a foot taller than her, but that was where the similarity to the young man she'd once known ended. This man was broader. Harder. She'd caught glimpses of the gentleman with whom she'd fallen in love earlier as she watched him smile and laugh with the other guests. But now, as he waited for her reply, he was guarded. The youth who'd once delighted in life was gone, replaced by the jaded individual standing before her.

Had his years in the army done that to him, or was she responsible?

Her eyes roamed over his face, looking for some

clue that would tell her what he was thinking. Well, at least he was no longer ignoring her.

She inclined her head, taking her cue about how to act from his own indifference. "Lord Cranston, is it not?"

He lifted one brow. "Come now, surely I'm not that easy to forget. I seem to recall a time when you quite enjoyed my company."

If he'd said those words to any other woman present, she knew there would be a hint of teasing in his tone. But with her, there was an edge of mockery to the statement. She spared a moment to glance away from him, afraid someone might have overheard him. Fortunately, they were alone. Well, as alone as one could be in a room that was still filled with people.

She met his pale green eyes again. The same eyes that greeted her every day when she looked at her daughter, a constant reminder of everything she'd lost.

She held her hands at her waist and took a steadying breath. "I didn't think you wanted to speak to me."

"I don't. But since it appears we now share a few acquaintances, I thought it prudent to get this first meeting out of the way." His gaze bored into hers for a few moments. "It seemed you were thinking the same thing, or was I mistaken in that? It certainly wouldn't be the first time I was mistaken about your motivations."

She felt this sting of his accusation and couldn't deny him the right to level it at her. He was correct after all. And when he learned what else she'd kept hidden from him, he would be more than cold. He'd be furious.

She licked her lips and noticed the way his eyes zeroed in on that brief motion before he met her gaze again. Heat coursed through her as she remembered how much she'd loved kissing this man. How much she'd loved him. But those days were gone.

It was impossible not to dwell on past regrets about how she'd treated Gideon—they were an ever-present companion. Still, she needed to be strong. She'd wronged him once, and she needed to make amends. "We need to speak."

"Is that not what we're doing now?"

She lowered her voice. "In private. There are matters we need to discuss."

He shook his head. "I have nothing to say to you outside of the polite courtesies I must show you when we are in public. And even then, I'd prefer if we agreed to ignore one another whenever possible. I'm only speaking to you now because I've caught the way the bride's gaze has been traveling between the two of us all morning. I wanted to ease her mind and, by extension, that of a very close friend." He took a step closer and his voice lowered further. "Do not mistake my attempt to ensure their wedding day remains a happy one for anything else."

He started to turn away. In a panic, knowing she wouldn't have another chance to speak to him, she reached out to touch his elbow.

Gideon froze in place. Several seconds passed before he turned back to her. Before he could give her a set down, she reached for a calling card she'd tucked into her glove after the wedding breakfast was over. She hadn't expected to give it to him today but had wanted to be prepared for the possibility.

She placed it in his palm. "Please. If you ever cared for me, even a little... If there is some small part of you that is still the man I once knew, call on me tomorrow. I will be home all day. It is vital that we speak. There are things you don't know about what happened all those years ago."

A muscle pulsed along his jaw, but he took the

card and placed it in a pocket of his tailcoat. "I make no promises."

And with that, he turned and strode away to join the newly married couple.

He was correct in saying that Mary had been watching them. He said something that caused the slight downturn of her lips to lift into a smile. Then she laughed.

Abigail had to turn away from the sight. If Gideon hated her now, he would detest her tomorrow. If he even called on her. But he needed to know that the love they'd shared had produced a new life. He needed to know that he had a daughter. What he chose to do after she told him would be his decision. She had no expectations of him. She'd lost that right a long time ago.

# CHAPTER 5

*A*bigail was already awake and dressed when the sun rose the next morning. She'd had a restless night and had long since given up trying to find peace in sleep. She'd called for her maid as soon as she heard the servants moving about the house.

She couldn't stop thinking about seeing Gideon again yesterday and had gone over every word they'd shared too many times to count.

It was also impossible to forget the way he'd casually charmed every woman present, in particular the ones who were unwed. Some had made no effort to hide the way they followed his every movement.

It had unsettled her to watch how he'd moved

from person to person with such ease. She couldn't deny that she'd hated seeing how easily he smiled and laughed with those other women. A spark of jealousy had ignited within her that refused to go away despite the way she'd admonished herself for the emotion. She had no right to Gideon's attention. Not anymore. She also needed to stop thinking about him as the young man who'd once loved her. He was Baron Cranston now and not Gideon.

The man's popularity had helped her in one respect yesterday. If anyone noticed the way she'd paid him a little too much attention, they would think her just another woman who hoped to catch his eye.

She found it impossible to relax as she made her way downstairs, her thoughts going over what she'd do if he didn't call today. She didn't want to keep trying to accost him in public so she could speak with him. As a last resort, she might need to visit him at his town house. She'd have to be discreet, but society looked the other way when it came to a mature woman's liaisons. She only hoped that if she had to go that far, she wouldn't run into another woman leaving his home.

She smiled as her daughter bounced into the breakfast room, the little girl's natural exuberance never failing to lift her spirits. Since it had always been just the two of them, Abigail had never bothered with the formality of having Gemma break her fast with the governess.

But as Gemma chatted away, Abigail became distracted and found it difficult to focus on what her daughter was saying. Every time she looked at the girl, she was reminded, yet again, of her father. How he'd looked at her with such cool indifference yesterday. So different from the way he'd looked at her when they were courting.

Holbrook had been furious when she'd begun to increase one month after they'd wed. The birth of her daughter five months later had confirmed what he'd already known to be true. That the baby she was carrying wasn't his.

She considered herself fortunate to have given birth to a daughter even when Holbrook cast her out of his house shortly after her confinement. Oh, he'd enjoyed her body while she was still with child, but after Gemma's birth, he'd sent her away to one of his lesser holdings. If she'd had a son, he would have made both of their lives a nightmare.

Before sending her away, her husband had told her that he wouldn't reward her betrayal by providing her with another opportunity to sire his heir. He'd promised her that when he passed away —and since he was already sixty-five when they wed, they both knew that day would come sooner rather than later—she wouldn't have any of the advantages that came from being the mother of the next Viscount Holbrook.

He'd meant it as a punishment, but sending her away had the opposite effect. Finally she was free. Her father had ensured she couldn't marry Cranston and had forced her to marry a man old enough to be her grandfather. But now she no longer had to suffer Holbrook's odious attentions.

When her husband passed away the previous year, she hadn't been shocked to learn he'd left her only a small yearly allowance. It would have been enough for her to continue living in a modest cottage somewhere in the country but little else.

Abigail had only been able to move into this house in London because her husband's heir was a good man. Shocked at his great-uncle's shabby treatment of her, the new Viscount Holbrook had settled a generous yearly sum on her.

"Mama, you're not paying attention."

Abigail smiled at her daughter. "I'm sorry. I was thinking about something I have to do later today. What were you saying?"

Gemma's brows scrunched together. "Are we still getting a kitten?"

One of their neighbors had a cat who'd just given birth to a litter and Gemma's heart was set on having one as soon as they were old enough to be weaned.

"Of course. The arrangements have already been made."

Gemma's face lit up with a smile that did much to lighten Abigail's heart. Whatever else happened —or didn't happen—they would always have each other. And now, with the new viscount's assistance, she wouldn't have to worry about ensuring her meager allowance stretched enough to cover all their expenses.

The governess came down to collect Gemma for her lessons when breakfast was over. Abigail hugged Gemma and watched her follow behind the middle-aged woman who'd been with them for the past four years.

The rest of the morning dragged. Abigail tried to work on some embroidery, but after pricking her finger for the third time, she gave up on the attempt and chose a book to read. When she found herself reading the same page over several times without comprehending what she'd read, she set the novel aside. She spent the next hour wandering through the small town house, looking for something, anything, that would hold her attention.

It was now early afternoon and Cranston still hadn't called. She'd just said goodbye to Miss Phillips and Gemma, who normally went for a walk after they had their luncheon.

She was beginning to despair, convinced that Cranston wouldn't be calling, when a knock sounded at the front door. Her fingers came to a stop on the keys of the pianoforte, where she'd been trying to soothe the despondency growing within her.

One minute passed before her butler, a kindly older man, stepped into the music room and held out a silver tray upon which rested a small card. Her hand shook when she reached for it.

With a deep breath, she glanced down to look at the name. Air rushed out of her lungs when she saw that it belonged to the new Viscount Holbrook.

With a smile of thanks, she asked the butler to arrange for tea and refreshments. She took a few moments to steady herself when he departed and then made her way to the drawing room.

The viscount rose to his feet when she entered. The man was only a few years older than her own twenty-seven years and quite handsome. At over six feet in height, he was taller than her husband had been. He had the same deep blue eyes as his great-uncle, but his hair was dark brown in color. Her husband's hair was already gray when they'd wed, but a painting that had been commissioned in his youth showed that his hair had been fair.

She dipped into a curtsy. "I didn't expect to see you today, my lord."

"I wanted to check on you before I left town. I will be departing for the estate in a week's time, and I hate the idea of leaving the two of you here without any family nearby."

She couldn't hold back her smile of amusement given how her husband had all but abandoned her after her first year of marriage.

It wasn't a surprise that, like most of the ton, the viscount was leaving London now that the social season had drawn to a close.

"We are both well. You needn't delay your departure on our behalf."

A footman entered with the refreshments. She thanked the young man and lowered herself onto the settee, then waited for the viscount to take his seat in the plush armchair before pouring him a cup of tea. He'd made it a habit to visit on occasion over the past few months, and she knew he drank it without milk or sugar. She handed the cup to him and then went about adding both to her own tea.

"Are you sure you and Gemma don't want to return with me? I know my uncle was less than generous, but the dowager house is yours to use whenever you'd like."

She was starting to shake her head when he continued. "Or the two of you can come down on your own later, once you've tired of London."

She smiled at him. "You are too kind. Your uncle would be rolling over in his grave right now."

It was no secret that Holbrook hadn't wanted his heir to take the two of them under his wing. She wouldn't be surprised if he'd gone as far as to leave instructions to that effect. But when she'd met her husband's heir, he'd vowed to would make up for the former viscount's neglect.

"My great-uncle was a miserly man who didn't deserve you or Gemma. It is unconscionable that he thought to punish you just because you didn't bear him an heir."

She'd allowed everyone to think that was the reason Holbrook had sent her away. She would hardly admit that her daughter wasn't Holbrook's.

"We have done well, the two of us. And to be

honest, I've spent far too much time away from everyone and everything. I've quite enjoyed being back in London."

He took one of the small sandwiches from the refreshment tray and popped it into his mouth. They made polite conversation for several more minutes before he finished the rest of his tea.

"If you change your mind, the invitation is always open. You need only send word."

"Thank you, my lord. If things don't work out here in London as I hope, I will reach out to you." The last thing she wanted to do was to leave London, but if her conversation with Cranston didn't go well, she might need to depart.

He couldn't hide his curiosity at her statement, but he was too polite to press further. He'd been very generous with her and Gemma, but she didn't know him well. Certainly not well enough for him to inquire about her plans.

"Thank you again for calling. Gemma is out with her governess, but I will let her know that you asked after her." Unlike the man the world thought was Gemma's father, the new viscount seemed to genuinely like her daughter. But then it was impossible not to become ensnared by Gemma's exuberant nature. Which was another reason she'd been glad to spend the past eight years away from her husband. She hated to think about how Holbrook might have mistreated her.

Their call at an end, she stood. Viscount Holbrook rose to his feet as well, and she followed him out into the hall.

He took his top hat from the butler and stepped outside, then stopped at the top of the stairs and turned to her. "I will be in touch to let you know when I'm leaving. Unlike my uncle, I'm not content to just abandon you to your own devices. You and Gemma are family."

Overcome with emotion at the unexpected sentiment, she placed a hand on his forearm. "Thank you, truly. Your generosity has been most unexpected."

He placed his gloved hand over her bare one and squeezed her fingers gently. Then, without another word, he made his way down the few steps and onto the street where his carriage was waiting for him.

She watched the conveyance pull away and was about to turn back into the house when a prickling under her skin had her glancing to the left. Cranston stood several feet away, casually resting one shoulder against a neighbor's house. Her breath caught in her throat.

He was watching her with a slight frown. From the tense set of his broad frame, she realized he'd seen her interaction with Lord Holbrook and he wasn't pleased. Did he think she was bidding a lover goodbye?

When he pushed away from the building, she feared he was going to turn and walk away. Instead, he stalked toward her.

# CHAPTER 6

Cranston struggled to push back his annoyance as he watched the pair's tender goodbye.

He knew that the tall, dark-haired man was the new Viscount Holbrook. He'd seen him often enough over the season, but he'd never paid him any attention. Well, the viscount had his interest now as Abigail reached for his arm and smiled up at him.

He couldn't help but feel as though he was witnessing history repeat itself. The interaction of the two people standing outside the door to her town house could have been innocent, but they were both young and attractive. It wasn't outside the realm of possibility that the viscount was Abigail's lover.

He told himself that the disappointment coursing through him wasn't because he'd expected to resume a relationship with Abigail. But it appeared she hadn't changed at all over the years. Had she invited him here today, hoping to play the two of them against one another?

He'd done his research before deciding to call on her. Her husband had left her with next to nothing, which Cranston could only assume was because she hadn't provided him with an heir. It was unusual, but there must have been something in their marriage contract that stipulated she provide him with a son. Abigail's husband was already over sixty when they'd wed, and he would have been desperate to secure his lineage. But she'd given him only a daughter.

Her town house was in a respectable neighborhood, however, so he could only assume the man now leaving her house had made those provisions for her.

His mouth compressed into a thin line as he tried to banish the unwelcome thoughts. It was entirely possible that the new Viscount Holbrook was simply acting with honor toward a woman who had been left destitute by his great-uncle. Perhaps he thought he was righting the wrong that had been done to her.

But Cranston no longer had it within him to give people the benefit of the doubt. Abigail had done that to him. Killed the optimistic young man he'd once been. He didn't think he'd ever be able to trust her—or any woman—fully again.

He'd done everything in his power to forget the day she'd broken his heart. And the past nine years serving in the army as they battled Napoleon had achieved that end. But since seeing her again the month before in Hyde Park, the memories refused to leave him.

Her father, the Earl of Hargrove, hadn't approved of Cranston's courtship. When Cranston had asked her about approaching her father for the man's permission to propose, Abigail had been the one to suggest they elope. It was the only way they'd be able to wed, she said.

So when he received a letter from her saying that she'd accepted another man's proposal, he'd made his way to her house, convinced she was being coerced into the match. Expecting to discover she'd been locked in her room, he'd gone first to the side of Abigail's London town house. He'd peered up at her bedchamber window, expecting to see her there, motioning in some way for him to come rescue her.

When the window mocked him with its emptiness, he made his way back to the front of the house and knocked. His muscles had tensed as he prepared to push past her family's butler and storm into the house and he'd been shocked when he wasn't turned away.

He hadn't anticipated he'd be shown into the drawing room where Abigail was waiting, a book in her hands. And then she'd turned his whole world upside down. She'd told him that she now agreed with her father that it would be in her best interest to make a more advantageous match.

Despite Cranston's certainty to the contrary, she'd made it very clear that she wasn't being forced to accept another's suit. And now she was a widow. Did she hope for another dalliance with him while she sought out her next husband?

When the viscount's carriage pulled away, she turned toward him. Had she already seen him, or had she sensed his presence the same way he always knew whenever she was near?

He made his way toward her, keeping his pace steady. When he reached her side, she stood as still as a statue. Her hands were gripped together at her waist. If he wasn't mistaken, his calm regard made her nervous. That observation improved his mood since it meant he wasn't the only one affected by this ill-advised meeting.

Neither of them spoke as he followed her into the house.

There was a strange moment when he met the butler's gaze. The man's eyes widened as though he recognized him, but Cranston couldn't remember meeting him. The butler was older, silver-haired, and of average height. Nothing about him stood out, so it was possible they'd met when the man worked in another household. Perhaps they'd met before Cranston purchased his commission.

Cranston waited while Abigail asked the butler for a fresh pot of tea. With a formal nod, the man removed the tray that currently rested on the table of the drawing room.

Abigail turned to face him then, her hands clasped at her waist again. "I wasn't sure you'd come."

He lifted one shoulder. "Neither was I, but curiosity overcame me. I couldn't imagine why you needed to speak to me. But apparently I'm not the only man to whom you've issued a similar invitation. How long do I have before the next man arrives?"

"I only invited you," she said as she sank onto the settee. "That was my late husband's heir, the new Lord Holbrook. He was calling to let me know he would be leaving town next week."

Cranston said nothing as he sat in one of the two comfortable chairs placed at right angles to the settee. Her admission should mean nothing to him, but he couldn't deny he was relieved. And he hated himself for that emotion.

Apparently, despite the way she'd broken his heart, he still wanted to think well of this woman. She'd led him to believe they had a future together, only to cast him aside with casual cruelty. He'd been made to feel like the worst sort of fool, but it seemed a small part of the young man he'd once been was still alive within him.

He blamed Ashford and Lowenbrock for that fact. Seeing his two friends happily married was giving rise to emotions and desires he'd never thought he'd feel again.

Silence descended as a footman brought in a new tea tray.

Abigail poured his cup and was reaching for the milk when he stopped her. "I drink it without adding anything now. We didn't always have luxuries in the army, and I quickly learned to do without." He didn't bother telling her that he also drank coffee now instead of tea.

She nodded and handed him his cup. He watched her closely as he took a sip and noted the way her hands shook slightly as she prepared her own cup before leaving it on the table.

She met his gaze and he waited. This was just another battle for him, and he was determined not to betray any weakness.

She gripped her hands together in her lap, no doubt hoping to hide the way they trembled, but he'd already seen it. His own hands were steady as he took another sip of the black, unsweetened tea before he placed his cup on the table.

He raised a brow, letting her know that it was up to her to start this conversation.

She let out a soft breath. "Thank you for coming."

He leaned back and waited.

"You're not going to make this easy on me."

He folded his arms across his chest. "Is there a reason I should?"

Her shoulders sagged. "You shouldn't."

He continued to wait, and after a tense silence, she shook her head.

"I don't know where to begin, but I did want to tell you that I never wanted to marry Holbrook. I very much wanted to marry you."

He couldn't hold back his snort of amusement. "I'm sure you didn't. If only the title I was in line to inherit one day wasn't so far beneath the daughter of an earl. Then you wouldn't have needed to marry someone old enough to be your grandfather."

She winced. "I was horrified when Father confronted me and told me that I had no choice."

Somehow he kept from swearing. "I don't believe you. You had to know that the young fool you'd so easily wrapped around your finger would have done anything for you. Anything."

She paled, but he was too angry now to stop.

"I'd planned to return in the middle of the night and spirit you away to Gretna Green if you'd given me any indication you were being forced into the marriage against your will. Instead, you called me a fool."

Her hands came up to cover her face.

"Come now, it's too late for acting. I'll admit

your theatrics once worked on me, but I'm no longer the same gullible youth."

She took a shuddering breath and lowered her hands. He was impressed to see that she'd managed to conjure up a tear. Clearly she'd had time to perfect her already impressive acting skills over the years.

"I had no choice."

He leaned back in his chair and waited for her explanations. But instead of continuing her attempts to convince him of something they both knew was a lie, she shook her head and drew in a shuddering breath.

"What happened that night no longer matters. Nothing we do or say now can change it. You wouldn't believe anything I have to say."

"No, I wouldn't. So then tell me, *Lady Holbrook.*" She winced at the use of her title and he continued. "Why am I here? If you're curious about how I've improved in the bedchamber, I'm sure I have an hour to spare before I move on to more important things."

She straightened her shoulders, unfazed by his attempts to wound her with his casual dismissal. "We have a daughter." Her words were rushed.

"Surely one of the servants can look after your

daughter. It's too bad you couldn't provide the old man with a son. Then you'd be at your estate right now instead of in this much smaller house." He leaned forward. "I know that Holbrook banished you from the estate to one of his smaller holdings. So tell me, was the sacrifice worth it? Did you gain everything you'd hoped for?"

Her breathing was shallow as she shook her head. "You mistake me. I don't mean that Holbrook and I have a daughter. I mean that you and I have one."

Silence descended as he found himself incapable of speech. She couldn't mean… No. His mind shied away from that possibility. Her child wasn't his. She was hoping to gain something from him with this lie. Money, no doubt, since he'd discovered she had very little of her own.

He stood, not caring that it was rude to do so first. "This meeting is over. I don't know what game you're playing at, but I don't believe you."

He turned to leave, cold fury washing over his body.

"Gideon—"

He whipped around to face her. "No!"

She froze, tears now streaming down her face.

"You lost the right to call me that years ago. I

am Baron Cranston now. The boy you could so easily manipulate in the past died the day you called him a fool for thinking he was good enough to marry you."

This time he made it all the way to the hallway when he was forced to stop. The front door opened and two people entered. A young girl and an older woman who was likely her governess.

The girl was laughing at something the woman said, and then she turned and looked at him.

The world stopped, and the only sound he could hear was the roar of his own blood in his ears.

The girl dipped into a circumspect curtsy before smiling up at him. "You have green eyes just like me."

He was staring down into a pair of pale green eyes that were identical to his own. And he realized then that Abigail hadn't been lying. No, this child was his. The same dark hair, the same eyes.

He turned to stare at Abigail, who called her daughter—no, their daughter—to her side and dismissed the governess with a small nod toward the stairs.

He had to get out of there. His thoughts were a jumble, and a tight ache had lodged in his chest.

He'd thought he'd already suffered loss but knowing that the woman he'd once loved had chosen to raise his daughter as another's was a pain beyond anything he'd ever experienced.

He fled from the house, unable to deal with this latest betrayal.

His daughter's words floated after him as he bounded down the three steps to the street. "Did I say something wrong, Mama?"

# CHAPTER 7

*C*ranston considered going to his empty town house and drowning himself in spirits until he could no longer think. Could no longer hurt.

Instead, he told his driver to take him to Mayfair. Ashford had already left that morning on his wedding trip with his new bride. And even if he hadn't, Cranston wouldn't impose on the couple during this special time.

But the Marquess of Lowenbrock was staying in London for now. His wife was with child and wasn't well enough to endure the long carriage ride back to their estate in Yorkshire.

The news of Amelia expecting hadn't really

come as a surprise to Cranston. It seemed he was fated to be surrounded by happily married couples while his own life continued to grow bleaker.

He was a regular guest at the house, and the butler admitted him without the formality of announcing his visit. He told Cranston that he would find Lowenbrock in the study.

"And Lady Lowenbrock?" he asked. The last thing he needed today was to walk into his friend's study and find the two of them in an embrace. Or worse.

"Her ladyship is resting. Should I ask a maid to inform her of your arrival?"

With a shake of his head, he thanked the man and made his way down the hall. He rapped on the study door and entered when John called out.

John leaned back in his chair, a grin forming. "I didn't expect to see you today."

By way of reply, Cranston moved to the sideboard where an assortment of spirits was laid out. He reached for a bottle of whisky and poured a healthy measure into a cut crystal glass.

John came around the desk to stand next to him. He could feel the man's eyes on him. "It's a little early to begin drinking. Has something happened?"

Cranston downed the contents of the glass and poured himself another before turning to meet his friend's worried gaze. "Congratulate me. Apparently I'm the father of an eight-year-old girl whom the world believes to be another man's child."

His friend's shock was unmistakable. He let out a soft curse and plucked the glass from Cranston's hand, then nodded toward the pair of comfortable chairs that were grouped together before one of the study's windows.

Cranston dropped into a chair and watched as John placed his drink on the sideboard. That was fine. He would speak to his friend first, and then he would drown out all memory of what he'd learned today. It would have to suffice for now until he figured out what to do about the grenade Abigail had thrown into his life.

John settled into the seat opposite him. They were silent for almost a full minute while his friend tried to find words for the situation. There were none, of course, and Cranston's eyes went back to the sideboard.

Finally John leaned forward, his elbows on his knees. "Tell me everything. I won't breathe a word to anyone if you don't wish me to."

Normally they didn't pry into one another's

personal affairs. They offered opinions, of course, but they didn't share private details of their dealings with the fairer sex. But Cranston couldn't ignore the bone-deep certainty that he needed to unload this burden. Share it so it was no longer his to bear alone. And when the time came, he'd allow John to tell Ashford. He didn't think he'd be able to tell this story twice, but he wanted both of his friends to know everything.

"You know about my past with Lady Holbrook." He gave himself credit for being able to say the name without wincing. It had taken a very long time—years, in fact—before he could even think of her as anything other than Miss Abigail Burton, the beautiful young woman he loved and with whom he'd planned to spend the rest of his life.

John nodded once. "Just what you told us that one time you drank a little too much."

He had vague memories of that night. It had been just after Ashford announced Mary had accepted his proposal. His real proposal. They'd been pretending to be courting before that day. Apparently Cranston couldn't think about the past without wanting to drink himself into oblivion.

"You said that you had a romantic interest in her before you enlisted," John continued.

Cranston let out a soft snort. That was a tepid description for what he'd felt for the woman who still had the power to tie his insides up in knots.

"After his marriage ceremony, Ashford told me that your wives were planning on promoting a match between us."

"That's true. Amelia told me that Mary thought it would be a good idea to see if they could bring the two of you together again. I don't know the details, but I do know that Ashford told her that wouldn't be wise." John leaned back and folded his arms across his chest. "Apparently that only made her more determined."

"Yes, and she invited the woman to their wedding breakfast."

John raised one shoulder. "I don't know what they're thinking. Amelia has assured me that they'll no longer be playing matchmaker. But she and Mary like her a great deal. It's possible she would have invited Lady Holbrook anyway."

Cranston tried to ignore the way his fingers itched with the need to hold on to that glass again. How much he needed to feel the burn of the amber liquid as it blazed a fire down his throat. He had to finish this conversation before he could get on with the business of getting well and truly drunk.

"We met during her first season. She was eighteen and I was twenty-one. Needless to say, I was young and stupid. It didn't take long before I fell under her spell. And I was foolish enough to believe she felt the same way about me. She accepted my marriage proposal, and I told her I would speak to her father."

"I assume her father turned you down."

"I never made it that far. She sent me a note that she'd accepted Lord Holbrook's suit and that she wished me well." He shook his head. "A fucking note."

He rose to his feet and walked to the sideboard with two long strides. John said nothing as he tossed back the drink that had been taunting him. He turned to face his friend again. The weight of the empty glass in his hand felt like a lifeline. "Two short lines that changed my life forever."

John said nothing for a few seconds before continuing. "You know this is how things are. Women don't usually have a choice about whom they wed."

"Of course I know that, which is why I went to see her. I expected to be turned away. To find she'd been locked away in her room. I was already thinking about how I could come back that night and spirit her away to Gretna Green."

John said nothing, merely waiting for him to continue.

Cranston turned to pour himself another measure of whisky. He didn't intend to drink it just yet, but watching the amber liquid swirl into the glass gave him a measure of calm.

"She was sitting in the drawing room, calm as can be. Waiting for me since she knew I wouldn't just accept her letter as the truth. And trust me when I say she gave me no indication she was being forced."

"That doesn't mean she wasn't."

"I might be able to believe that if she hadn't laughed at me. Told me that she'd decided she'd much rather be a wealthy viscountess—one who was no doubt going to be a widow soon—than bind herself to someone who would one day be a baron with little in the way of wealth or possessions to recommend him."

Anger flared in John's eyes. "So Amelia and Mary are wrong about her."

Cranston took a swallow of the drink, savoring the burn. The alcohol was already starting to dull his senses, so he needed to slow down. "It's possible she came to regret her actions. My curiosity overcame my better judgment, and I looked into her current situation. Apparently, shortly after they married, Holbrook banished her to a small estate in the north and behaved as though he were never wed. I'd assumed he was disappointed she'd given him a daughter. That he could no longer perform in bed and had no use for her. But now I think he was angry when he realized he wasn't the father."

He lifted the glass and examined the way the light streaming through the room's windows played on the cut glass, causing the liquid within to sparkle. He was about to down the rest of the drink but John was faster. His friend took the glass from his hand and set it just out of reach. Damn, his reflexes must already be affected.

"So she told you that you are her daughter's father. How can you be sure she wasn't lying?"

"I saw her." His throat was suddenly dry, and it took more than a little effort to continue. "She has my eyes."

John swore.

One corner of Cranston's mouth quirked up, but he couldn't bring himself to laugh. Nothing about this situation was amusing. "I agree. Now can I have the rest of my drink?"

John led him back to the chair he'd vacated, and he actually stumbled. Damn, that whisky was quite good. Cranston would have to ask his friend where he could get some since he suspected he'd need it again in the future. It normally took more than two and a half drinks before he started to feel a drink's effects.

He dropped into the seat without protesting. John watched him for a moment, no doubt assessing whether Cranston was going to leap back out of his chair again. When he remained, John settled back into his own chair.

"Before your thoughts become too clouded, you need to consider what you're going to do now."

Cranston barked out a laugh. "I'd hoped to completely obliterate all rational thought so I wouldn't have to think about it anymore."

The frown on John's face told Cranston that he was serious. He and Ashford had begun calling John Sir Galahad when they were all serving together in the army because the man was incapable of seeing a woman in jeopardy without wanting to rush in and offer his assistance. He supposed that gallantry also extended to trying to help his friends.

Cranston scrubbed a hand over his face. "To be honest, I'd hoped that today's meeting would be the end of my association with the woman. That I'd be able to put her firmly in the past. But now…"

"Now you've learned you have a daughter."

Silence stretched between them. Cranston leaned back in his chair; his eyes closed as the girl's face swam into his mind. She had his eyes. He was fairly certain that Abigail's husband hadn't had pale green eyes. If he were thinking clearly, he'd make arrangements to confirm that fact. But everything inside him was already screaming at him to accept the truth. He had fathered a child with Abigail and then purchased a commission and fled England. If he'd known Abigail was carrying his child, he never would have left. He would have moved heaven and earth to bind the woman to his side.

"Are you going to see them again?"

Cranston swore. They both knew the answer to that question. Of course he was. He'd just learned he had a daughter, had caught only a brief glimpse of her, but already every one of his instincts was screaming at him to protect her. To ensure she didn't slip away from him the way her mother had.

He squeezed his eyes shut as he realized exactly what he needed to do. The only way to ensure the girl could remain a part of his life was to bind her—and Abigail—to him.

He opened his eyes and met John's steady gaze. Apparently his friend already knew what he was going to say. "She's my daughter, and she's been without a father's love up to this point. I aim to remedy that situation."

John nodded. "I would expect nothing less. And Lady Holbrook?"

Cranston's teeth ground together. "I'm not going to give her another chance to escape. It's clear that she wanted me to know my daughter. Whatever else she might think of me, she knows I would never abandon my child."

"You intend to marry her."

Cranston rose and moved to the sideboard. "And this time she won't be able to escape me." He downed the rest of his drink and poured another.

"I'll arrange to have a room prepared for you tonight and will send word to your valet that you'll be here. I have a feeling you'll be needing that room soon."

His friend left the study, but Cranston knew he'd be back soon. He didn't mind that John had just appointed himself his caretaker. After all, why else would he have come here? They'd had to watch each other's backs often enough during many battles. He could drown his anger without fearing he'd be set upon while drunkenly trying to find his way home.

# CHAPTER 8

It was ironic that the only friends Abigail had made since arriving in London just before the end of the season were the wives of Cranston's best friends. Amelia, the Marchioness of Lowenbrock, and Mary, now the Viscountess Ashford. The latter was on her wedding trip with her new husband, and so Abigail had invited Amelia to visit.

Abigail couldn't risk calling upon the marchioness if there was a possibility Cranston would be there. Their last two meetings hadn't gone well. The man she'd once loved—whom she still loved—had ignored her for most of the wedding breakfast, and then yesterday…

She closed her eyes and took a deep breath, but the scene refused to leave her mind.

Cranston had been furious with her. Angrier than he'd been the day she'd told him she was marrying someone else. The look he'd given her had made it clear he would never forgive her for this betrayal. For raising his child as that of another man. It didn't matter that she hadn't known at the time that she was with child because she never should have allowed her father to force her into turning Cranston away.

That was two days ago. She'd spent all day yesterday waiting for some word. A visit, a letter, something. Instead, the day had crawled by. She hadn't slept well last night, and by morning her nerves were scraped raw.

She was picking half-heartedly at the keys of the pianoforte when there was a knock at the door. It would be the marchioness, of course, but that didn't stop her foolish heart from leaping into her throat.

She didn't wait for the butler but made her way to the front entryway, where the man was closing the door behind Amelia.

Neither said a word as she led her new friend into the drawing room and Amelia swept her into a quick hug.

Abigail winced. "How much do you know?"

Amelia shook her head. "Nothing. Cranston called two days ago, and he spent the night at our house. He was drinking heavily, and my husband didn't want him to leave in that condition."

Abigail lowered herself onto the settee, and Amelia sat next to her. "I assume your husband knows what happened? And he didn't tell you?"

Amelia shook her head. "They served together in the war. There is a bond between them, and Ashford as well, that will never be broken. And since I assume whatever Lord Cranston shared didn't have anything to do with me, my husband wouldn't betray his confidence. But..."

Abigail could only look at the woman. Her lack of sleep must have muddled her thoughts because it was clear the marchioness expected her to know what she'd left unsaid. She could only shake her head in confusion.

"If the matter concerns you, there is nothing to stop you from telling me. Perhaps together we can come up with a solution. Or at least some way to make things easier for you and the baron."

Abigail was sorely tempted to do just that. But in the end, she shook her head. "If Gideon... I mean Lord Cranston... wanted you to know, he would have shared. Or he would have allowed your husband to share the details with you. I owe it to him to respect that decision. I've already taken so much away from him."

It didn't matter that her father had well and truly compelled her to his will. Nor did it matter that she'd acted in what she'd thought was Cranston's best interest at the time. Making excuses for her actions wouldn't change the fact that he had lost so much. She only hoped he wouldn't allow bitterness to keep him from becoming acquainted with Gemma. He'd already missed far too much of her young life.

She leaned back against the cushions of the settee and closed her eyes, the hopelessness of her situation an oppressive cloud hanging over her. "I shouldn't have asked you to visit today. I was being selfish. I don't want to place you in the middle of something that could cause difficulty between you and your husband."

"Nonsense," Amelia said.

Abigail opened her eyes and met the woman's gaze.

"I know firsthand just how stubborn men can be," Amelia said. "Women need the comfort and support of a friend during these times even when there are no easy solutions to be found."

Warmth filled her chest, and she sat up again. "And if I'm the villain?"

Amelia's head tilted to one side. Somehow Abigail kept from flinching under the woman's close examination.

"Is that true?"

Abigail let out a breath. "Yes? No?" She shook her head. "It doesn't really matter. Cranston will always see me that way, especially now."

Amelia wrapped one arm around her shoulders. "I think you need a distraction. Tell me, can you be trusted to keep a secret?"

Abigail knew what the woman was doing. Amelia wanted her to know that she'd be safe confiding in the marchioness, and what better way to do that than by sharing a secret of her own?

"I am the queen of keeping secrets." Truer words had never been spoken.

Amelia's smile was enigmatic. "Do you know that I like to write?"

Abigail shook her head, confused. "Letters?" She didn't have anyone with whom to correspond, but she looked forwarded to doing that with Amelia when the woman left London.

The marchioness's grin widened. Her voice was low when she said, "Novels."

Abigail almost thought the marchioness was being dishonest when she confided that she was the author of *A Fallen Lady*, the most popular novel in London at the moment. Perhaps in all of England. No one knew who'd written the book, but it seemed that everyone had a theory.

"Is that true, or are you trying to distract me?"

Amelia laughed. "Oh, it's true. And it's very amusing to listen in to everyone's theories about the author."

Abigail shook her head in wonder. "I haven't read it yet. I want to, but I'm waiting for new copies to arrive at the bookstore. They keep selling out before I can claim one for myself."

Color touched Amelia's cheeks. "I have extra and can give you one. But please do me the favor of telling me you haven't read it yet if you discover you don't like it."

Amelia's distraction worked, and for the first time since seeing Cranston again at the wedding breakfast, Abigail's thoughts weren't centered on the man. She called for tea, and Amelia shared the background of how she'd come to write the story.

When the clock on the mantel chimed one

o'clock, Abigail reached for one of the woman's hands and gave it a quick squeeze. "Thank you so much… for everything."

Amelia patted her on the knee. "John and I went through a difficult time as well, and I feared everything was lost. But in the end, we were able to come together and are now happier than ever."

Abigail sighed. "There is no happily-ever-after in store for me and Cranston, but I hope we can reach a point where we are on friendlier terms. If only for… Well, it would make everything much easier."

Good heavens, she'd almost told Amelia about Gemma. So much for her assertion that she could keep a secret. It seemed that telling Cranston the truth had opened the floodgates, and now the truth wanted to come spilling out of its own accord.

If the marchioness noticed her near misstep, she said nothing. When they rose, Amelia engulfed her in a hug. "Please let me know if you need anything. I understand why you don't want to come to the house, but I can visit again." She placed a hand on her belly. "I'm increasing and early mornings have been rough for me of late. So have long carriage rides, hence why we are remaining in London for the time being."

Abigail embraced the marchioness again and offered her congratulations. "Being a mother has been my greatest joy in life. I wish only the same for you."

She was in much better spirits as she watched Abigail leave. Nothing had changed with respect to her situation with Cranston, but it helped to know that she had a true friend. More than she would have imagined.

Another knock at the door several minutes later had her smiling again. She was waiting in the drawing room doorway when the butler opened the door.

"Did you forget…?" Her words died when she saw that her visitor wasn't Amelia returning to collect something she'd forgotten.

Instead, her gaze collided with Cranston's, and in his eyes she saw a steely determination that had her stomach swooping from nerves.

"Please join me," she managed around a suddenly dry throat.

She watched him give his hat to the butler, her eyes drinking in his broad shoulders and the dark hair that was just a little too long. And then, when his gaze met hers again, those pale green eyes. The same color as their daughter's.

She dropped onto the settee, and Cranston lowered himself into the same armchair he'd sat in on his last visit. She hadn't been sure she'd ever see him again.

They were silent as they watched the butler remove the tea tray from her visit with Amelia.

"I can send for a fresh pot if you'd like." Her voice was low and she cleared her throat. She could certainly use another drink.

But Cranston shook his head. "I'm not staying long."

He waited for the butler to leave, but his eyes remained fixed on hers. She couldn't tell if he was still angry. He seemed grim, but the anger she'd seen two days ago was gone. Perhaps that meant they could discuss the situation without any harsh words.

"I know my news was a shock, but I felt you needed to know."

His lips pressed together before he said, "Nine years later?"

She flinched under the accusation. "I was already married when I learned that our… time together had caused me to fall with child. I knew you'd already purchased a commission and were no longer in London, so I couldn't reach out to you.

And even if I had been able to, neither of us was in a position to change things."

She held her breath as she waited for his reaction to her words. When he nodded, she let out a soft breath. Something that felt akin to relief flittered around the edges of her mind. Perhaps things would work out. He could come to know Gemma, and Abigail would be able to see him from time to time. It was the best she could hope for.

His next words turned her world upside down.

"We'll get married of course."

# CHAPTER 9

Grim satisfaction swept through him as he watched shock take hold of the woman who was always destined to be his wife. Her eyes widened, and all color drained from her face.

"I didn't…" She wet her lips and took a deep breath before starting again. "That wasn't why I told you about Gemma. You can see her whenever you'd like."

He rose, crossed over to the room's door, and closed it quietly. His own shock had worn off since learning the truth two days ago. He'd spent yesterday nursing one of the worst headaches of his life, but it had given him time to think about how he wanted to proceed.

Abigail's staff would soon learn everything—he was almost certain her butler had already guessed the truth about Gemma's true parentage—but he wanted privacy for this conversation.

When he turned to face Abigail again, he took the time to examine her closely. He didn't think she was lying. He'd well and truly taken her by surprise. But that didn't mean she wouldn't try to turn the situation to her advantage.

"I am not content to play the role of an occasional visitor in her life. So unless you plan to relinquish custody of her to me, my plan is the only logical course of action."

Her expression was so transparent he could almost see the thoughts flit through her mind. It hadn't occurred to her that he'd want custody of his child. Which left one question: Would she take this opportunity to cast the girl aside and return to society, unfettered by the obligation of motherhood? The woman he'd once thought her to be would never do such a thing, but he'd been so wrong about her then.

He closed the distance between them. This time he took a seat next to her on the settee. Not close enough to touch her, but he could tell that his proximity unsettled her further.

She licked her lips before speaking, and it took every ounce of willpower he possessed not to look down at her mouth. But that didn't mean he could hold back the memory of how much he'd once enjoyed kissing her.

"Tell me, *my lord*. Are you proposing this just to punish me? Like my first husband, will you also be sending me away after we've wed?"

The bite in her tone only served to tell him that he'd made the right choice. "I won't take Gemma's mother away from her. If you decide not to accept my offer, that decision will be yours, not mine."

"This isn't what I would call an offer. It's an ultimatum."

He lifted one shoulder. "You can have your freedom."

Her face set in determination, her fear seeming to evaporate. "Never. I will never abandon my daughter. If you insist on taking her, you'll need to take me as well."

Somehow she made it sound as though she were the one making this decision and not him. That fact should annoy him, but it didn't. It spoke to the love she had for her daughter. Their daughter. She might only have been pretending to love him all those years ago, but it was very clear that the woman sitting next to him, arms folded across her chest and a scowl on her face, loved the child they'd created.

"Then it is settled. I will have my solicitor call tomorrow with the marriage contract. If there are any changes you wish to make, you can let him know. As long as they're not too outrageous, I'll have no issue accommodating them."

Her eyes widened in surprise. "That is very generous of you."

"I do have one condition that I insist upon."

Her shoulders straightened. "Of course. What is it?"

"You are to remain faithful to me."

Her eyes—those beautiful blue eyes he'd once loved to gaze into—sparked with anger. "I've only ever lain with two men. You were the first and my husband was the second. There's been no one since he sent me away within a year of our marriage."

He nodded. That fact shouldn't have meant anything to him but he couldn't ignore the relief he felt. He told himself it was only because he wouldn't need to worry about her passing off another man's child as his.

"But tell me, my lord"—her words dripped with false sweetness—"do you intend to do the same?"

He wanted to laugh. What right did this woman have to demand he remain faithful when she'd so easily cast him aside for another?

"That will depend entirely on you. As long as I don't tire of our bed sport, I see no reason I'd need to look elsewhere."

Her mouth dropped open before she snapped it closed. "I didn't think that we… that you would want to…"

He leaned into her space. "What good is a wife if I can't fuck her?"

She flinched at the crudeness of his words, which was exactly the reaction he'd hoped for. But then it was his turn to be shocked when she leaned closer.

She stopped when her lips were just an inch from his. "Then you'll need to teach me everything I must do to keep your attention."

Fire flooded through his veins, and he took her mouth. He'd meant to control the kiss, to punish her, but it was clear from the moment their lips touched that neither of them was in control.

Their mouths moved together as though they were both starving. That shouldn't have been true for him—heaven knew he'd had his share of lovers since returning to England—but it was. Not one of those other women mattered to him, just this woman in his arms. The one he'd lifted to sit across his lap without even realizing he was doing it.

His thoughts were ablaze, his cock harder than it had ever been in his life. He ground her backside against his hardness, enjoying the soft little mewl she made in the back of her throat. Her fingers threaded through his hair, and it was clear she wasn't going to stop. He could have her right here on the settee.

He would have to be the one to pull away. He didn't want their first time together again after all these years to be like this. Out of control and filled with passion. If he was going to maintain control in their marriage, he needed to find a way to gain the upper hand over his errant lust for Abigail.

Lust that had apparently only intensified over the years.

She made a soft sound of protest when he tore his mouth from hers. When she tried to close the space between them again, he placed his hands on her shoulders to stop her.

"I don't think we'll have any difficulty with the physical side of our marriage."

His voice wasn't quite steady, but she didn't

seem to notice. When he released her, she slid off his lap and sat next to him.

"I apologize for getting carried away." She wouldn't meet his eyes.

He took her chin between two fingers and turned her to face him. "I don't know if I have it in me to forgive you for what happened in the past, but there is no reason we can't move forward. We were scarcely more than children then, but we've both grown."

She nodded, her slight smile tremulous. "Of course."

There was a soft knock at the door, and Cranston moved to the chair.

Amelia bade the person to enter, and the door was opened by the butler. He gave no indication that he was scandalized by the fact Amelia was entertaining a gentleman behind closed doors.

If Cranston was correct in his assumption that the man had already guessed he was Gemma's father, he'd know they'd been intimate in the past. Still, a small part of him couldn't help but wonder if this was a regular occurrence with Amelia. It was possible she hadn't been truthful with him about her lack of sexual experience.

He hated the way jealousy clawed at his belly at

the thought and tried to dismiss his doubts. He'd have heard rumors if Abigail liked to entertain men privately. But it bothered him that his feelings toward her weren't entirely in the past. If he truly thought she was lying to him, he should be feeling anger and not jealousy.

"Excuse the interruption, my lady, but Miss Phillips was wondering if you'd be joining them this afternoon."

A hint of heat crept into her face. "Of course. Please tell her I'll be up shortly. And let her know that I wish to introduce the two of them to someone."

"As you wish, my lady." He left the room with a small bow.

Cranston rose to his feet when Abigail stood. She took a deep breath, and he resisted the temptation to glance down at her breasts. The ones that had been pressed against him just moments ago.

Damn, he had to drag his thoughts away from that or he'd be hard for the rest of the day.

"About the wedding," he said, returning to the practical matter at hand. "I was thinking we could have it in one week's time."

Her brows drew together. "So soon? I thought you'd want to wait until Lord Ashford was back from his wedding trip." Her frown deepened. "Will he be returning to London after that, or will they be staying in the country?"

He wanted to take her into his arms and ease that frown from her face. Instead, he clasped his hands behind his back. "Ours isn't a love match, so there's no point in waiting. He'll understand." Ashford would be shocked to learn about his marriage, but he wouldn't be hurt. His friend knew that Cranston had little interest in romantic nonsense.

She nodded. "I understand. Will Lord and Lady Lowenbrock be there?"

He couldn't imagine being able to keep them away. "I'll invite them, yes."

She seemed relieved at the idea. Which made him wonder about just how close Abigail had become with his friends' wives.

"Then there's only the matter of introducing you to Gemma. If you'd like, we can do that now."

He'd known this was a possibility today, and logically there was no point in putting off the introduction. Still, a small part of him worried that his daughter wouldn't like him, especially after their first meeting.

"You don't want to tell her first and then introduce me later? It will come as a shock."

Abigail smiled. "Gemma likes to meet people. She's asked me several times about the man who visited the other day."

He grimaced, remembering how curt he'd been. "I hope she doesn't hate me."

"I told her that you were late for another appointment and had to leave. She accepted the explanation."

He let out a breath. "Are you going to tell her who I am?"

He expected her to say no. To make some excuse about how his daughter would need to adjust to his presence in her life first before she told Gemma the truth. But she surprised him by nodding.

"I think the time for lies is behind us." At his frown, she amended, "Behind me. I think anyone who knows her can tell just by looking at you that the two of you are related. I don't want her to be the last person to learn the truth."

Her hands were clasped at her waist, the knuckles white. He closed the distance between them and placed his hand over them. "She'll be shocked, but young children are better able to take these things in stride."

She took a deep, shuddering breath and nodded.

He dropped his hand. "It is my understanding that Holbrook wasn't a father to her. Is that correct?"

"He never saw her after he sent us away. She had no reaction when she learned about his death. I don't think the concept of him as a father was ever real to her."

That eased his fears somewhat. "Then lead the way."

# CHAPTER 10

She'd gone over this decision countless times. Gemma was still young, only eight years of age. She wouldn't fully understand just how much her life was about to change, but Abigail believed it would be for the better.

And Cranston. She glanced at him again as she led the way upstairs to the large room at the back of the house that was used as a schoolroom. The tense set of his jaw told her that he was nervous about this meeting.

Gemma would be finished with her lessons and had wanted Abigail to join her and Miss Phillips for their afternoon walk. Abigail hadn't exaggerated when she said that Gemma loved meeting people. She also loved surprises. Abigail only hoped she would come to accept Cranston as her father just as easily.

Abigail took a deep breath when they reached the door and opened it. Gemma was sitting at a table, drawing, and she looked up with a wide smile at her mother's entrance.

She dropped the pencil and ran to her mother's side. "Can we go for our walk now, Mama?"

Abigail crouched so she was level with her daughter. "In a few minutes. But first I would like you to meet someone."

Gemma's eyes had been trained on hers, but now she looked up at the man who had entered the room behind her.

"You're the man who visited the other day." She dropped into a curtsy.

"It is a pleasure to make your acquaintance," Cranston said with a formal bow. Then he grinned at the girl and Gemma giggled.

Abigail's heart lightened as she took her daughter's hand and led her away from the doorway. She turned to Miss Phillips. "You can meet us downstairs in ten minutes."

The governess dipped her head in acknowledgment and turned to leave. But Abigail caught the curious glance she cast at Cranston.

And so it began. Soon the entire house, and then all of London, would know the truth. She hoped they could protect Gemma from the speculation, but society wasn't normally kind when they discovered a juicy bit of gossip. While her daughter wasn't illegitimate, news that Abigail had passed another man's child off as belonging to her husband would soon be on everyone's lips. At least most of society had already quit town. She only hoped that another scandal would already be making the rounds when the next season started.

Abigail led Gemma back to the table where she'd abandoned her drawing and sat next to her at the table. Cranston remained where they'd left him, just inside the doorway, and she appreciated the way he was allowing her to take the lead. Another man would have blustered in, full of demands. But then again, she never would have given her heart to that type of man. Gideon had been kind and thoughtful, and she was happy to see that his years away at war hadn't erased that young man completely.

"I have happy news to share. This is Baron Cranston. We knew one another many years ago when we were both younger. And…" She licked her lips, uncertain how to proceed. Gemma didn't need to know all the details, but Abigail had to tell her something that would explain why they were getting married so quickly.

"And we were in love."

They both looked at Cranston, who had come to join them. He crouched so he was looking Gemma in the eye. "Your mother and I were in love with each other, but things happened and we were separated. She married another man and I joined the army."

"Yes," she said, her voice cracking on the word. "But now he is back, and we have come to realize that we would like to marry. Soon. Next week."

Abigail's eyes roamed over Gemma's face, trying to decipher what her daughter was thinking. The little girl looked away for a moment, and Abigail was almost afraid she'd have one of her rare tantrums.

"I hope that meets with your approval. I asked your mother to marry me, but now I am asking you, as well, if you'll agree to it. I can wait if you want to get to know me better first, but I'd very much like to become a family."

Abigail's heart threatened to crack. The expression of earnest hope on the man's face had her realizing, yet again, just how much she'd taken from him.

Gemma's eyes narrowed on Cranston. Then she raised one hand and brought it to the corner of one of his eyes. "Are you my real papa?"

Abigail sucked in a breath, stunned. She searched for something to say, but Cranston took over.

"Would that make you happy?"

Gemma nodded. "I know that Father wasn't my papa. The servants would whisper about it."

Gemma's voice was remarkably even for the gravity of the information she'd just shared. Abigail hadn't realized her daughter knew anything about why they didn't live with Holbrook.

Cranston engulfed the girl's hand in one of his and gave a nod. He swallowed before continuing, and it was clear he was overcome with emotion. "I am your father, yes."

"And you want to be a family? Can we all live together?"

Cranston met her gaze, and she could tell he was remembering the past. The way Abigail had cruelly pushed him away because she'd known it was the only way to keep him from coming back.

But he'd never believe she'd done it to stop her father from ruining Cranston's family.

"If you will have me, yes."

Gemma's mouth widened in a broad smile. "I would like that very much."

Cranston's gaze shifted to her. Abigail didn't realize she'd started to cry until he reached out and flicked away the tear that was tracing a path down her cheek.

Gemma kept her grip on Cranston's hand as she reached for Abigail's with her other hand. "We're going to be a real family." She tilted her head to one side as she gazed at Cranston. "Should I call you Papa?"

He laughed. "Perhaps after I marry your mother. Can you wait one week?"

She blew out an impatient breath. "Are you coming with us on our walk today?"

"Oh no, Baron Cranston has other places to be—"

"I'd be delighted to join you and your mother."

Abigail's mouth closed with a snap. It would seem that Gemma already had her father firmly under her spell.

Together, they made their way downstairs. Miss

Phillips was waiting for them by the front door, and Gemma dashed to her side.

The governess smiled down at her charge. "You seem to be in high spirits."

"Can we tell her the news, Mama?"

Abigail laughed. "Since I doubt you could keep it a secret without bursting, I think we must."

She introduced the governess to Baron Cranston and then added, "I have accepted his proposal of marriage."

"We're going to be a family!" Gemma added. "And the baron is coming with us on our walk today."

"I'll let you know when we're back," Abigail said.

Miss Phillips reached out for her hand and squeezed it. "I'm very happy to hear the good news." She turned to take in Cranston as well. "My best wishes on your marriage," she said with a slight dip of her head. Then she turned and headed back upstairs.

Gemma was almost bouncing with excitement. Before coming to London, she would have grabbed her mother's hand and dragged her from the house. Abigail had hated to quash the girl's enthusiasm by telling her that she needed to behave with more decorum while they were in London. But it was impossible to quell her daughter's spirit entirely, something for which Abigail was grateful.

"Shall we?" Cranston held out his hand.

Gemma beamed at the two of them before taking his hand and then reaching out for her mother's as well. As they left the town house, Abigail suspected it wouldn't be long before Gemma chose Cranston over her. That thought should have left her dreading the future, but she couldn't wait to see it. From the way Gemma kept smiling up at Cranston, she knew that future would be happening soon.

# CHAPTER 11

When Cranston arrived at White's the next morning, John was already there. His friend was seated next to one of the unlit fireplaces in the morning room, reading one of the newspapers that were made available to members of the club.

"I wasn't sure you'd be here," Cranston said, settling into an armchair.

John folded the broadsheet and placed it on the mahogany side table. "Amelia was tired and wanted to rest. She's a curious mix of energy and exhaustion of late."

"How is she faring?" Now that he was to be wed, Cranston realized that before too much longer, he might also find himself with a wife who was increasing. The thought should have made him run in the opposite direction, but all that had changed when he met Gemma.

"She's been feeling better. We might yet be able to make it back to Yorkshire before the summer is over."

"But you'll still be in town next week?"

John lifted one shoulder. "We have no plans to quit London just yet." He examined Cranston closely. "I know you were planning to visit Lady Holbrook yesterday."

Cranston had almost forgotten he'd told his friend about his intentions for his visit. Their conversation had been three days ago, and it hadn't taken him long to become well and truly foxed. He'd collapsed into one of Lowenbrock's spare bedchambers. The following morning, he'd had to make his way home with one of the worst headaches of his life. Every bump of the carriage, despite the fact that the Lowenbrock carriage was well-sprung, had sent jolts of pain straight through his skull.

"I was useless the next day. Barely made it into my darkened bedchamber."

"You certainly kept me busy trying to keep your

drinking from leading you into a stupor from which you'd never recover."

Cranston winced as he remembered how a mutual acquaintance had done just that. It was just after the final battle at Waterloo. Most of the men who'd survived and who hadn't been taken to a field hospital had all dropped into a bone-weary slumber.

The next day they'd celebrated. Lieutenant Bradford was one of the men who'd escaped unscathed, only he'd been haunted by all the bloodshed they'd witnessed during that final battle. It was the oddest thing. The young man had been fine up until that point, able to keep his emotions at bay. But once the war was over and Bradford realized he'd be returning home soon... He'd drunk so much that night that after he passed out and was carried to his cot, no one could wake him the next day.

Cranston hadn't known one could die from imbibing too many spirits. No doubt that was why some internal instinct had led him to his friend's house after learning about Gemma. He'd known John would watch out for him and ensure he didn't suffer a similar fate.

"Given how I felt the next day, I appreciate your efforts."

After a short silence, John let out a huff of breath. "Are you going to tell me what happened?"

Cranston wanted to ask for a drink despite the fact it was so early. But memories of Bradford's death had him forcing back the impulse. Instead, he called one of the footmen over and ordered a coffee.

His friend waited with barely restrained patience.

"I saw her yesterday."

John leaned forward. "And?"

"I offered and she accepted."

Cranston drank from the cup the footman had just placed on the small table to his left and watched the frown form on his friend's face. He was fairly certain John was torn between congratulating him and telling him he was making a mistake.

But John was an optimist by nature. He'd always assume that things would work out for the best. He might not be happy about the circumstances surrounding Cranston's upcoming nuptials, but he'd hope for a good outcome.

John nodded. "I hope that one day the two of you will be able to remember how you used to feel.

Nothing good can come from dwelling on the unpleasantness of the past."

Cranston could wholeheartedly agree with that. He'd purchased a commission to escape his heartbreak and now had reentered ordinary life to escape the horrors of all he'd seen and done during his time at war. He needed to leave all that behind him and move on. They'd both seen what happened to those who were unable to do that.

"Tell me," his friend said, "did you meet your daughter?"

Cranston didn't even try to hold back his grin. "I did."

"I take it she's fine with her mother's upcoming marriage?"

Cranston shook his head in wonder. "She's incredible. Whatever else I might think about her, Abigail is a very good mother." He still couldn't believe how his visit yesterday had gone. "Gemma guessed that I was her father."

John's eyebrows rose at that unexpected detail. "Because of your eyes? Surely that's a large leap in logic for a child to make."

"She told us that she'd overheard servants talking about how she wasn't Holbrook's daughter. After learning about my plans to marry her mother

—and Abigail shared we were once in love—it didn't take much for her clever mind to put the pieces together."

John crossed his arms over his chest and smiled. "I never thought to see the day when a member of the fairer sex would so fully ensnare you."

Cranston barked out a laugh. "She did do that, and I never saw it coming. She wasn't even trying—she was just being herself."

"What happens now?"

"For the immediate future, the wedding is planned for next week. I already procured a special license after leaving their town house yesterday. And I have my solicitor drawing up the marriage contract. I hope you and Lady Lowenbrock can be there."

John inclined his head. "Of course. It's a pity Ashford won't be here, but I can understand why you don't want to wait."

"After all the times I called him a fool for wanting to wed Miss Mary Trenton, I can just imagine what he'd say." His cynicism had caused him to be less than kind to his friend. "I do wish them well together. I hope he believes that."

"I'm sure he does. And he would wish the same

for you. Although he might give you a hard time about it."

"One I'd very much deserve," Cranston said. "I hope Abigail and I can come to an agreement and make a happy household for our daughter. Or at the very least, one filled with little strife." His mouth twisted. "Gemma wants us to be a 'real family,' whatever that means. Hopefully it will be enough that we live together under the same roof and don't argue."

John shook his head. "Eight years old and already making demands. You're going to have to be careful not to spoil her."

Cranston raised a brow. "Are you telling me you don't plan to spoil the child your wife is currently carrying?"

John winced. "We both might be doomed."

They laughed, and much to his surprise, Cranston realized he was looking forward to the future. The thought sobered him a little. He needed to be careful or he would be in danger of repeating past mistakes. He needed to guard his heart because recent events had made it clear that a small part of the foolish, optimistic youth he'd been all those years ago was still buried somewhere deep within.

He'd have to make sure that part of himself stayed buried.

John glanced toward the door of the room and leaned toward him. His voice was low when he spoke. "Holbrook just arrived. Should we introduce ourselves?"

Cranston recoiled at the thought. He could still remember the way the man had looked down at Abigail while taking his leave that day. The way she'd placed a hand on his arm and smiled up at him.

They'd both seen the man before, but they'd never been introduced. Perhaps it was best to keep it that way.

"The decision has been made for us," John said. "He's heading this way."

Cranston steeled himself for whatever would happen. And he refused to consider that his newfound hostility toward the viscount, who was much younger and far more handsome than the previous Viscount Holbrook, had anything to do with jealousy.

Holbrook reached their table and bowed. "Cranston, Lowenbrock. I know we haven't been formally introduced, but may I join you?"

John waved toward the free chair that was next

to his.

There was something about the set of the man's jaw that had Cranston's instincts on high alert. He knew without being told that Holbrook was here to discuss his upcoming marriage to Abigail.

Cranston gave John a subtle look that his friend easily deciphered.

John stood. "If the two of you will excuse me for a moment, I see someone I need to speak to. I'll be back in a few minutes."

His friend had only taken two steps when Holbrook got straight to the reason for seeking him out. "The dowager viscountess informed me of your upcoming nuptials."

Cranston raised a brow. "I take it you don't approve?"

Holbrook folded his arms across his chest, his brows drawing together in a scowl. "My great-uncle was less than kind toward her. As I am his heir, she is currently under my protection. I would like to know your motives for moving so quickly. It was my understanding that you have no problem bedding every widow in London. I never expected to hear you'd actually propose marriage to Abigail."

Cranston's teeth ground together at the viscount's use of her Christian name. "We were acquainted many years ago. I even courted her then, though she did not accept my suit. I believe she came to realize that was a mistake."

Holbrook made a soft sound of disgust. "I've met Gemma. Knowing what I do about your reputation, I can well imagine how that *courtship* went." He leaned forward, his hands settling on his knees. "If you hurt her again, I'll call you out."

Every muscle in Cranston's body tightened, and he had to take a deep breath to hold back the haze of anger that threatened to cloud his vision. The nerve of the man was galling. If Holbrook had hoped to keep Abigail for himself, he'd be doomed to disappointment because Cranston was never letting her go again.

"If you must know, it was the opposite. I was the young fool who wanted nothing more than to marry her, but she cast me aside to marry someone else." He kept his tone even, but the threat was clear in his voice. "That won't be happening again. So if you were planning to keep her for yourself, you should know that I'm very good with both a pistol and a blade. If you're so eager to meet your death, just name your weapon and your second."

Holbrook leaned back in his chair again and

just stared at him. Cranston refused to be the first to look away.

Finally, one corner of the man's mouth lifted. "Fair enough. I just needed to ascertain she wasn't rushing into another marriage that would end unhappily... both for her and for Gemma. As she is the Dowager Viscountess Holbrook, I would have ensured her comfort. But I'm glad to see you mean to be there for her now. And for Gemma as well."

Holbrook leaned forward and offered his hand. Despite wanting to plant his fist in the man's face, Cranston shook it.

Holbrook stood and strode from the morning room. Cranston stared after him, a sense of unease settling over him. Where the foreboding came from, he couldn't say. It seemed that Abigail hadn't been lying to him about Holbrook's motives. Unless Cranston's instincts were completely wrong, he sensed there would be no interference from the viscount.

And the fact that her father hadn't been in London this past season meant there would be no interference from the Earl of Hargrove. Rumor had it that the man was ill, possibly even on his deathbed. Abigail's father had already meddled once, and Cranston had no doubt he would have continued to do everything in his power to ensure that Cranston never married his daughter.

Cranston made a mental note to do some more digging into the past. Because despite his hardened heart telling him that Abigail wasn't to be trusted, he had a sense that there was more to this situation. His instincts about people were rarely wrong, with Abigail being the only exception to that rule.

But perhaps she wasn't an exception. It was possible that his initial assumption that she was being coerced when he'd received her letter breaking their betrothal had been correct.

John dropped into his chair. "I take it your conversation went well?"

The corners of his mouth lifted. "He threatened to call me out. But have no fear, you won't be called into duty as my second anytime soon. We've managed to come to an agreement about my upcoming marriage."

John grimaced as he took another sip of the coffee that had no doubt gone cold in his absence. "From everything I've heard, he doesn't seem to be a blackguard. I imagine he's acting out of a sense of duty."

Cranston's lips pressed together as he met his friend's gaze. "You have connections."

John's brows rose. "As do you."

He leaned forward. "One of your sisters is very good friends with Brantford's wife."

Brantford, who was once known as the Unaffected Earl, had been thought to have ice water running through his veins. But his marriage, and his very obvious affection for his wife, had shown the world that the impossible was true. That the man had a heart buried somewhere beneath that icy exterior.

"Catherine, yes. They're very close."

"Brantford has connections everywhere. He has no reason to help me, but perhaps you can convince your sister to reach out to his wife. I need to know exactly what happened in the past to make Abigail marry Holbrook. If her father had something over her, I need to know what it was."

# CHAPTER 12

Abigail spent the next day in a strange mood. A large part of her still couldn't believe Cranston had asked her to become his wife. He was doing so because of Gemma, of course, but it was an outcome she'd never thought would happen.

When she'd decided to seek him out and tell him about his daughter, she only wanted to give him the opportunity to get to know her. And of course she'd known that Gemma would get much out of their relationship. Gemma had spent her whole life with a father who was one in name only. And now that the former Viscount Holbrook had passed and Cranston was no longer in military service, the time had finally come to tell them both the truth.

But to have him propose marriage? No, while she might have fantasized about such an outcome on occasion, she'd never expected it to happen.

It was impossible not to dwell on the kiss they'd shared. The way his mouth had consumed hers, the feel of his hard body against hers. The hard length of his arousal against her hip that told her he wanted her just as much as she wanted him.

She'd had to drag herself out of her musings several times as she went about the practical business of preparing for her upcoming marriage.

As her first task, she sent a short letter to the new Lord Holbrook to let him know about the development and to thank him for going out of his way to look after her and Gemma. She hadn't wanted him to worry about the two of them remaining in London after he left town. When he'd replied later that day, she expected his congratulations and to learn that he would hasten the date of his departure. She suspected, after all, that he was only remaining in town to give her the opportunity to change her mind about returning to the country seat with him.

What she didn't expect was for him to call on

her. He was with her when Cranston's solicitor arrived with the marriage contract. He'd also accompanied her to consult with his own solicitor to review the agreement before she signed it.

And then this morning she received an invitation from the Marchioness of Lowenbrock to join her on a shopping trip. Abigail readily agreed, of course. It would be far more enjoyable to visit Bond Street with a friend. She'd gone alone, with only a maid for company, when she'd first arrived in town and needed to purchase a new wardrobe that wasn't composed entirely of mourning colors.

She wondered if Cranston had already told Lord Lowenbrock about their upcoming marriage and if he, in turn, had shared the news with Amelia. He couldn't keep their wedding a secret for long, but it would be a blow to discover he was hiding it from his friends until the last possible moment.

After breaking the fast with her daughter, she left Gemma in the very capable hands of Miss Phillips just as the Lowenbrock carriage was slowing to a stop in front of the town house. Abigail rushed out of the house to save Amelia the effort of having to come collect her.

She climbed into the Lowenbrock carriage to find Amelia smiling widely at her.

"Thank you for accepting my invitation today despite the weather. I hope it doesn't start to rain while we're out."

Abigail took in the luxurious interior of rich red leather as she settled next to her new friend. She leaned back into the plush seat cushions and sighed. As the carriage pulled into the street, she could already tell it would be a far smoother ride than the small, modest carriage she'd rented for her stay in town.

"It was a wonderful surprise to hear from you. I know you said that mornings weren't good for you, and I remember how difficult they were when I was increasing."

Amelia grimaced. "Yes, but fortunately today has been going well. No queasiness at all." She gave her head a small shake as if to dispel the memories of unpleasant mornings. "That's enough talk about such distasteful matters. I plan to visit all my favorite shops today while I still have the energy."

Abigail sighed, tension already leaving her body. "It's been so long since I've enjoyed such an outing with a friend. I haven't done this since I married Holbrook."

Amelia patted her knee. "Have no fear, I will introduce you to every store—and everyone—you'll need to know. My husband's sisters are surprisingly well connected. Of course, some of those introductions will need to wait until the start of the next season since so many have already left London." She tilted her head to one side. "Is there a reason you chose to arrive in town just as the season was drawing to a close?"

Of course the marchioness wouldn't know the details of her situation. Just another bit of proof that Cranston never spoke about her aside from any confidences he might have shared with Amelia's husband.

"June marked the one-year anniversary of my husband's death, so I was officially in mourning until then. I saw little point in arriving earlier since I wouldn't be able to attend any of the events." She hesitated a moment before continuing. "Also, my father has been unwell, so I was visiting with him this spring."

And of course her father had spent much of that time lecturing her about what she needed to do to keep her next husband happy. He even had a list of men he thought would be appropriate.

She shouldn't have been surprised. None of the

men on that list were as old as her husband had been, but they were all almost as old as her father. Now that Abigail had a measure of independence, thanks in large part to her husband's heir, she would never again let her father dictate her life choices.

When her father didn't press the matter beyond presenting her with that list, she suspected his illness must be more serious than he wanted everyone to know. She thought he'd let the subject of a future marriage drop.

Then her brother had informed her that Father was making arrangements to have Lord Graven-hurst visit, with an eye toward seeing a marriage contract with the twice-widowed baron signed before his death. Her brother had advised Abigail to leave for London as soon as possible.

She'd intended to wait until the start of the next season before rejoining society, but with the knowl-edge that her father was still trying to control her, she felt no guilt about saying her goodbyes and departing. Honestly, she wouldn't be surprised if the man was just pretending to be ill in an attempt to get his own way. She only hoped her brother wasn't experiencing similar attempts to force him into a marriage of their father's choosing.

"I'm sorry to hear that," Amelia said.

Abigail smiled her thanks and murmured something about how her brother had remained behind to oversee the estate while their father was ill.

Amelia blew out a breath. "Well, since you're not going to mention it... My husband told me about your upcoming wedding to Lord Cranston."

Abigail met her gaze, half expecting to find censure there. Instead, she saw only curiosity. "It was most unexpected... Did he tell you the reason for his proposal?"

Amelia nodded. "Yes. He told my husband that he could share the information with me. But John told me little beyond the fact that Cranston is your daughter's father."

Abigail let out a soft sigh. "That's something of a relief. I was afraid he would try to hide it. If for no other reason than to spare my daughter the gossip that is sure to arise."

Amelia shook her head. "Lord Cranston is a good man even if he is something of a rake."

Abigail moved past that last comment. It bothered her more than a little to think about the very real possibility that her future husband might take a mistress, or at the very least continue with his affairs.

"They have the same eyes. Anyone who sees the

two of them together will guess that he is her real father."

"How is your daughter—Gemma, is it not?—dealing with the news of your marriage?"

"Honestly?" She let out a soft chuckle. "She's over the moon with excitement."

Amelia smiled. "I know that Lord Cranston has much experience charming the fairer sex, but I never imagined it would be so easy for him to win over a child. So he is good with her?"

"He is incredible." Her throat clogged and tears sprang to her eyes. She had to take a deep breath to steady herself before she could continue. "I feel so much guilt about keeping the two of them apart for all this time."

Amelia's gaze softened. "Did you know you were with child when you agreed to marry your husband?"

She couldn't help but feel another twinge of guilt. "Of course not. My father made it impossible for me to consider Cranston's suit." She blew out a breath. "We'd planned to elope, but my father saw to it that I would never do that. Still, if I'd known, I would have taken the risk and fled with him to Scotland even if it would have led to our ruin." She leaned forward and grasped Amelia's hand. "You must believe me. I never would have fallen in line with Father's plans if I'd known I was already carrying Gideon's child."

Amelia squeezed her hand in reassurance. "For what it's worth, I believe you. But I'm not the person you need to convince."

Abigail clenched her hands together in her lap. "I'm not sure that's even possible. I have no proof of my father's schemes, and whatever I say would be seen as a feeble attempt to excuse my actions— one he won't believe. I've already told him that I was left with no choice, but I don't think he believed me. In the absence of concrete evidence to the contrary…" She shook her head. "I think it best if we just look forward and make the most of our lives together now."

Her friend was silent for a moment. Then she said, "Lord Cranston doesn't believe in love. But unless I'm mistaken, I think you do. And that you're in love with him."

"I never stopped loving him. And yes, I know I caused him a great deal of pain. This whole situation with Gemma only makes it that much worse. I don't expect him to forgive me for the past." She shook her head to clear it of her maudlin thoughts.

"Please tell me that you and your husband will be there for the wedding."

"Of course. I'm only sad that Mary won't be there as well."

"Lady Ashford is on her wedding trip, and unlike my marriage, hers is a love match. It would only make her sad to see our hastily done-up affair."

"Well, I do have a confession to make."

Abigail wondered at the sly grin on the marchioness's face.

"Mary was the first, and now that you're the second, I can say that I seem to have developed a habit of taking my friends dress shopping. I do believe that it's turning out to be one of my most favorite traditions."

Abigail shook her head in confusion. "That's hardly a confession since I already knew we were going to visit Madame Argent. I will admit that I'm excited to see the inside of her shop. She was out of my price range when I first arrived in town. She still is, but perhaps I'll find something I can afford to purchase."

"We're going shopping for you, silly goose. We're buying you a new dress for your wedding and everything you could possibly need for your trousseau."

Abigail could feel the heat creep into her face. She'd be lying if she said she hadn't been thinking about what the physical side of her marriage would be like. She'd only been with Cranston that one time when they'd conceived Gemma. While the experience had been enjoyable, the pain had dulled the pleasure a little. It had also been a hurried affair since they were both afraid of being caught after slipping away during the last ball of the season. Cranston had assured her that their time together would be more enjoyable in the future since she no longer had her maidenhead. But they'd never had the opportunity to be together again.

Her couplings with her husband, before he'd banished her from his sight after she gave birth, had been even worse than that first time with Cranston.

But the way Cranston had kissed her when he proposed... He'd ignited every fiber of her being. A heat had risen within her that she'd never experienced, and she'd wanted him with a desperation she hadn't thought she would ever experience.

But she needed to be practical. "I still cannot afford Madame Argent's prices. But perhaps you can help me find some things at another modiste's shop."

Amelia waved a hand. "Nonsense. I've already told Cranston that I was taking you to the dressmaker today and that he would be paying the bill." She touched shoulders with her, her grin widening. "Trust me, the two of you will thank me for this later."

# CHAPTER 13

The rest of the week sped by with a flurry of activity. But the one daily constant was Cranston, who came to spend time with Gemma. It filled Abigail's heart with joy to watch the two of them grow closer.

When he wasn't there, Gemma peppered her with questions about their future. Would he come live with them or would they move into his house? Would they stay in London? Could they still adopt one of the neighbor's kittens when they were old enough to be separated from their mother? And the question that broke her heart—would they live together forever or would they have to live in separate houses one day?

Abigail did her best to assure her that when they

became a family, they would stay together. And she would do everything in her power to ensure that came to pass. Even if Cranston couldn't love her again, she would be everything he could want in a wife. Not just for her daughter's sake but for her own as well. Now that the universe had seen fit to give her a second chance with this man, she wouldn't squander it.

It did worry her that Cranston's demeanor toward her remained aloof. Much to her disappointment, there was no repeat of the kiss they'd shared after she accepted his proposal. That fact had her worrying about their wedding night. She wasn't very experienced in the ways of lovemaking. She knew the basics, yes, but she also knew there was more to it than just lying there and allowing a man to take pleasure in her body. If Cranston didn't guide her on what he wanted from her in the bedchamber, would she be able to keep him from seeking his pleasure elsewhere?

She considered asking Amelia for advice but in the end was too embarrassed to broach the subject. She would just have to see what happened first. The marchioness had already stressed that it was important she wear one of the special nightdresses they'd ordered on their shopping trip if she wanted to fully ensnare Cranston's attention. The garments had begun to arrive shortly after visiting Bond Street, and she'd blushed when she thought of her maid packing the daring slips of fabric away. She only hoped they would help in setting the right tone for her wedding night.

The morning of her wedding to Cranston dawned bright and clear, if a little cooler than normal for summer. Abigail wasn't one to give credence to signs, but she couldn't help but think it was a fitting metaphor for their upcoming marriage. Full of promise but with more than a hint of coolness between her and Cranston.

Viscount Holbrook had insisted on sending his carriage for her that morning. She thanked the butler, who was smiling fondly at her and Gemma as he held the town house door open for her. Today would be the last time she left this house as an unwed woman. She and Gemma had only been in town less than two months, scarce long enough to grow attached to their new home, but a part of her would miss it. She attributed the strength of that emotion today to her uncertainty about the future.

During one of his visits, Cranston told her how Holbrook had sought him out and that her husband's heir had even threatened to meet him at dawn if he hurt Abigail. She knew that Holbrook was only going out of his way to protect her and Gemma because he wanted to make up for how his great-uncle had neglected them.

But she couldn't deny that hearing the annoyance in his tone when Cranston relayed the details about that discussion gave her a sliver of hope about the future. She held on to the memory of the flash of what she hoped was jealousy that she'd seen in his eyes that day, telling herself it was proof that his feelings for her might not be dead after all.

She climbed into the carriage after Gemma, and they were followed by Miss Phillips. Gemma's governess was charged with looking after her daughter during the ceremony, and Abigail saw no point in sending her in another carriage.

Gemma was bouncing in the seat next to her. Miss Phillips opened her mouth to admonish her charge about curbing her exuberance, but Abigail smiled at the older woman and shook her head.

"It might be best to allow her to expend some of her excess energy now, before we get to the chapel." She looked down at Gemma. "Where you *won't* be bouncing in your seat."

"No, Mama," Gemma said before wrapping her short arms around Abigail's waist.

She dropped a kiss onto Gemma's head, careful not to muss the artful array of dark curls. Gemma's hair had a natural wave to it, so it hadn't taken long to create the hairstyle. Gemma wouldn't have had the patience to sit still if that weren't true.

Gemma looked particularly lovely that day, her coloring contrasting with her white dress. Abigail's own dress was a pale gold color, only slightly darker than her fair hair, which was also swept up in curls that had taken a great deal more effort to create. Abigail's hair was normally straight, and she hated how long it took with the heated tongs to curl her hair, but she'd sat through the ordeal because she wanted to look her best today.

Her hand went up to finger the double strand of pearls at her throat. She'd been surprised when a delivery from Cranston had arrived early that morning. Her hands had shaken when she opened the small, elaborately wrapped package topped with white ribbons to find the necklace nestled within on a bed of dark silk along with a pair of delicate pearl earrings.

As she stroked the small beads, she couldn't help but wonder if he'd sent the jewelry as a gesture of his willingness to give their marriage a real chance or if he'd sent them because he hated the idea of her wearing jewels her deceased husband had given her. He couldn't have known that she possessed no such jewelry.

Whatever his true motivation, she chose to take it as a sign that their union would be a happy one. Today she would begin her life anew, and finally she was on the path she should have taken all those years ago.

It was a short trip to the chapel, and soon the carriage was slowing to a stop. Abigail took a deep breath, expecting… something. Butterflies in her belly, the feeling that her heart was beginning to race. Instead, she was filled with a bone-deep certainty that she had made the right choice in accepting Cranston's proposal.

She turned slightly on the carriage bench and hugged Gemma tightly. "I love you," she said, allowing the embrace to continue a little longer than normal. After today it would no longer be just the two of them. Gemma's father would now have an active role in her life.

Finally she pulled back and smiled down at her daughter. "Be sure to mind Miss Phillips." She watched as the pair stepped down from the carriage with the assistance of a footman.

"I love you, Mama!" Her daughter's words

floated back into the carriage as the two made their way into the chapel.

Holbrook replaced the footman at the carriage door and held out a hand. "Are you ready?"

She nodded, her sense of certainty continuing as she took his hand and allowed him to help her down.

He'd surprised her when he offered to walk her down the aisle. Once again, she would be forever grateful for his show of support. If her father had been well enough to travel to London, he likely would have boycotted this wedding. He could no longer force her hand, but that didn't mean he would support, or respect, her wishes. Still, she wished that her brother could have been here.

This would be a small, private wedding. Aside from Holbrook, Gemma, and Miss Phillips, the only other guests were the Marquess of Lowenbrock and his wife. Amelia was standing with her while the marquess was acting as Cranston's best man.

She looked up at Holbrook. "Is everything ready?"

He nodded. "I sent the footman inside to inform them your carriage has arrived. They should be ready for you."

From the way he scanned her face, she guessed

he was looking for any sign of doubt on her part. It felt strange that this man, whom she'd known for less than a year, should care more about her feelings than her own father had shown when he'd forced her to wed the man of his choosing.

She smiled at him. "Then we shouldn't keep them waiting."

She placed her hand in the crook of his arm, and together they entered the chapel's vestibule. As he'd told her, they were already waiting for her. The footman who'd accompanied the carriage held the inner door open.

Unlike with her first marriage, she felt only a sense of anticipation. She was finally getting what she'd wanted all those years ago when Cranston was courting her. She could only hope it wasn't too late.

As they made their way up the short aisle, her gaze remained fixed on Cranston. Gideon. There could be no other man for her, and she made a silent vow to make the most of this second chance. He was only marrying her because of Gemma, but she would do everything in her power to make him happy. Cranston might never come to love her again, but it would be enough if he was content in their marriage. She loved him enough for the two of them, and she would make this work.

When she reached the front of the chapel, Holbrook handed her over. Before turning to face the clergyman, she took a moment to scan Cranston's face. But he kept his features carefully neutral, and it was impossible to decipher what he was thinking or feeling.

When he repeated his vows and placed the ring on her finger, she finally detected a hint of emotion. It was fleeting, and if she'd blinked in that moment, she would have missed it, but it was enough for her. For that look told her that he, too, was remembering their past. He was thinking about the wedding they should have had a long time ago.

When the service was over and they'd signed the register, he took her arm and they began their walk back down the aisle.

She leaned toward him, and he lowered his head to catch her whispered words. "You won't come to regret this."

His eyes met hers for several seconds before he looked away. He said nothing as they left the chapel.

# CHAPTER 14

*You won't come to regret this.*

Those were the first words she'd spoken to him after they were officially husband and wife, and he wasn't sure he believed them. He wanted to, but a part of him hated the fact that circumstances and their shared past had conspired to force him into this marriage.

But he would do it again to become a part of his daughter's life.

He was intensely aware of Abigail's presence in the confines of his carriage. He tried not to think about the kiss they'd shared and how much he wanted to drag her into his lap and get started on the wedding-night celebrations.

She looked like an angel with her blond hair

and gold dress, and he wanted nothing more than to debauch her. Ruin her for any other man.

Instead, he held his tongue as the carriage took them to his town house, where a short wedding breakfast would be held. He'd considered omitting the practice altogether since theirs was hardly a typical marriage, but he wanted to see Gemma today. She'd be going home with her governess afterward and would move into his house on the morrow. So if he wanted to spend any time with her today—and he'd made a point to see her every day since their introduction—he needed to invite their wedding guests back to the house.

There were also matters he needed to discuss with Abigail, but that would have to wait. He couldn't start the conversation on the carriage ride, and they'd no sooner arrived at his home than people began spilling out of their own carriages.

There was his friend John and his wife, of course. He knew that Abigail had grown close to the Marchioness of Lowenbrock in the short time they'd known one another.

Not that long ago, he would have assumed John's wife was trying to punish him in some way by seeing to it that his life was as uncomfortable as possible. But somehow he'd softened recently because he honestly didn't think Amelia had it in her to act with such malice.

And that fact worried him. His life was spinning out of control. He was starting to question long-held beliefs that all members of the opposite sex weren't to be trusted. That they could lead you to think they were deeply in love with you and then turn at the drop of a hat and cast you aside with casual cruelty.

He'd thought that somehow John had managed to find the only honest woman to be had, and given the man's disposition for rescuing damsels in distress, he counted his friend fortunate not to have fallen into the snare of someone who would manipulate him for her own gain.

But then Ashford had married Mary Trenton. He liked the woman well enough, had found her to be clever and levelheaded. Still, he'd been concerned that his friend was headed for heartbreak of his own when they were courting.

That hadn't happened. Instead, the two seemed genuinely to care for and, dare he admit it, love one another. And if Miss Trenton—or rather, the Viscountess Ashford now—had any nefarious motives, he had seen no sign of it.

And now there was Abigail. The Earl of Brantford had managed to unearth things about the past that Cranston hadn't known. Circumstances had come to light that made him question everything. He needed to speak to the woman who was now his wife, and he itched to send everyone away so he could do that now.

He found his eyes drifting toward her time and again while the small group of people who'd been with them at the chapel chatted and laughed together. Aside from the Lowenbrocks, there was only Gemma, Miss Phillips, and the infernal Lord Holbrook, who seemed intent on testing Cranston's patience.

Cranston hated how he felt the need to watch Abigail more closely when she was speaking with Holbrook, but he could detect no signs of a relationship between them beyond friendship and mutual respect.

Gemma flitted from her mother's side to his and tugged on his arm. He crouched down next to her.

She leaned in close and whispered in his ear. "When can I start calling you Papa?"

He touched a finger to her nose, grinning at the request. "You may start now if you'd like. But only if you feel comfortable doing so. I don't want you to do it because you feel you should."

Her expression was serious as she considered his words. "I think I'm ready… Papa."

Oh yes, his friend had been correct. This child already had him completely wrapped around her little finger.

"What's happening over here?"

They both looked up to where Abigail was standing, smiling down at the two of them. She looked exquisite, and the happiness that radiated from her gave her beauty an ethereal quality.

Gemma leaned against his shoulder. "I was just talking to Papa."

He watched Abigail closely, studying her reaction to Gemma's casual willingness to share their relationship with the world.

Abigail put one hand on each of their shoulders. "I'm so glad to see my two favorite people in the world getting to know one another better. We'll have more time to do that starting tomorrow. But for now, our guests are waiting for us to proceed them into the dining room."

Cranston rose to his feet. He held out an arm to his wife, who tucked her hand into this elbow, and took his daughter's hand. The heart he'd thought permanently hardened was starting to develop a few cracks, and that realization terrified him.

IT WAS A SMALL GATHERING, ATTENDED ONLY BY those who had been at the chapel. Not at all like the wedding breakfast held after Viscount Ashford's wedding. Abigail did her best to focus her attention on Gemma and on their guests and not think about the night ahead.

Cranston went out of his way to spend time with each of their guests. Abigail was aware of how differently he behaved with them. With Gemma he was sweet and patient. With Lowenbrock and Amelia, it was clear that they were on friendly terms because he was more open, no hint of reserve in his demeanor. And when he spoke to Gemma's governess, she could see that the older woman had also fallen under his spell.

He was polite and reserved when he spoke to Lord Holbrook... and to her. She wondered if everyone else could see it, but if they did, they were polite enough to pretend not to notice.

After the meal was over, Holbrook took his leave. Amelia and Lord Lowenbrock announced their plans to depart as well.

Amelia pulled her aside. "I know this is difficult

for the two of you, but I have confidence that things will work out in the end."

Abigail tried not to wince. "I'm holding on to that hope."

Amelia pulled her into a tight hug, whispering into her ear, "Don't forget to wear one of those special nightdresses later tonight."

She couldn't hold back the blush that rose to her cheeks as she thought about the scandalous scraps of fabric that Amelia's modiste had designed for her. Her trousseau had already been delivered to the house, so Abigail knew they were waiting in her new bedchamber.

Her blush remained as she said goodbye to Amelia and her husband.

Finally it was time to hug Gemma and assure her daughter that she would be coming to stay here on the morrow. Gemma didn't understand why she had to wait one more day, but fortunately Miss Phillips stepped in to tell her that they still had to visit the neighbor's kittens today. They were almost old enough to leave their mother, and Gemma hadn't chosen which one she wanted to adopt.

The additional reminder that her favorite doll was also waiting for her in their current home and might be left behind if Gemma didn't bring it with them tomorrow was enough to convince Gemma it was best to wait one more day.

Abigail stood back and watched Cranston give his daughter a hug, telling her that he looked forward to her coming to live with him.

He'd arranged to have two burly footmen accompany the carriage on its return. One month ago he hadn't known Gemma existed, but now he seemed to hate the thought of her being without her parents for even one night.

He stood on the front steps as the carriage pulled away, then shook his head. "I should have asked Lowenbrock and his wife to look after her tonight. I know they wouldn't have minded. Maybe I can send word for them to fetch her later—"

Abigail tugged on his arm and turned him away from where he stood, watching the carriage as it disappeared from view.

"Gemma will be fine," she said as the butler closed the door behind them. "The staff adores her, and her governess sleeps in the room next to hers. She'll hear Gemma if she has a nightmare."

Cranston frowned as he followed her into the now empty drawing room. "She has nightmares?"

Abigail shrugged. "On occasion, but they're not a common occurrence. I'm sure the only thing keeping her up tonight will be her excitement about coming to live with you."

He stared at her, his gaze boring into her very soul. Finally his head tilted to one side and his voice lowered. "And you?"

Her hand fluttered to her chest. "What about me?"

He took a step closer. "Are you excited about coming to live with me?"

She wanted desperately to say yes, but uncertainty gripped her. So instead, she took a step back.

"I am happy to be here, yes. But…" She shook her head, feeling more than a little silly. "I don't know how to proceed."

He arched a brow and she blushed. "I'm not referring to *that*. What I mean to say is that I'm not sure what you want me to do. I assume you'll want me to oversee the running of the household. Should I meet with the housekeeper now? She'll know your preferences, and I don't plan on changing anything—"

Her mouth snapped closed when he let out an impatient laugh.

"Perhaps you should sit down and take a breath. The house isn't going to fall into chaos if you don't take control this very minute. And there are other things we need to discuss."

She nodded and moved to the plush settee covered in dark green velvet, where she perched on the edge of the seat. A long time ago she'd dreamed of being in this house as Gideon's wife. She shouldn't be feeling nervous now that it had finally happened.

She waited for him to speak, content to allow him to lead this discussion.

He settled into a matching armchair. "I've had some time to think since you walked back into my life and turned it upside down."

She closed her eyes briefly. She couldn't deny that his description of their reunion was accurate, but her motivation hadn't been a calculated one. She'd only wanted to right a wrong. "I—"

He held up a hand and she stopped. "I wasn't making an accusation. I was simply stating the truth."

He leaned back in the chair and she waited, her nerves stretched taut.

"Not long after I entered military service, I received a letter from my mother. She was very distraught because my father's luck had turned at the gambling tables."

She froze. What did he know? She'd always assumed he was unaware of the extent of his father's gambling losses that spring.

"She told me that they were going to lose this town house. That he'd gambled it away. But apparently that never came to pass. She sent another letter soon after to tell me that everything had been settled."

He steepled his fingers, his eyes boring into her. She tried not to flinch under that steady gaze.

"At the time I thought she'd misunderstood the situation. Or that she'd exaggerated and painted circumstances as being dire to convince me to give up my commission and return home. Father liked to gamble, but he always knew when to quit."

She licked her lips. "I'm pleased to hear that. And clearly, since you're now in possession of this house, that never happened."

He didn't drop the subject. "I've looked into the matter this past week. When I returned to England, I vowed to leave the past behind me and think only about the present. But finding out I was a father changed everything. I needed to know the truth behind what happened all those years ago. With my family and with you."

Her heart was beginning to race now. "You could have asked me."

"True. But we both know I wouldn't have believed anything you told me. You've already lied to me so well in the past, only I couldn't be sure about what. Were you lying when you told me you loved me and that you wanted to spend the rest of your life with me? Or were you lying when you said that as someone who would only ever be a lowly baron, I wasn't good enough to wed?"

His words stabbed her like a dagger to the heart because they were true. She had lied to him. "I never lied about loving you."

He was silent for almost a full minute, and she feared her heart would burst out of her chest. Finally he nodded. "I believe you."

His words should have brought her happiness, but his tone was flat. Her worst fears had been realized. That even if he knew—and believed—the truth, it would no longer matter.

"But that doesn't change anything."

"I can't go through that again, Abigail. You've already crushed my heart once. I won't give it to you again. No, that's not true. I *can't* give it to you. That part of me died the evening I lost you."

She'd told herself that nothing she said or did

would change the way Cranston looked at her now. But in truth, nothing could prepare her for the pain lancing through her at his words. Again. He'd lost her all those years ago, yes, but she'd also lost him. And now she was losing the last of her hope.

She straightened. *No*, she thought. She couldn't give up. She wouldn't. Cranston was here, and she'd seen how he was with Gemma. He loved her and he had no qualms about showing it to the world, which meant that his heart wasn't as hard as he wanted her to believe. Perhaps he thought his words were true, but they were already on this path, and she needed to see it through.

"Will you believe me if I explain what happened all those years ago?"

He considered her words. Finally he lifted one shoulder. "I'm willing to listen."

She nodded and took a deep breath. "Father knew about my fondness for you. What I told you that night—about how someone who would one day be a baron was far beneath the daughter of an earl…" She shook her head. "Those were his words, not mine."

He remained silent, his arms folded across his chest.

She continued. "He went out of his way to

ensure I married someone else. I think he had his heart set on me capturing the attention of a duke or a marquess. When that didn't happen, he decided that a wealthy viscount would suffice."

"He didn't care that the man he chose for his daughter was older than him?"

"Apparently not. When I protested, he told me it was likely that I'd be a widow soon. At any rate, he came to me and told me that he'd learned about your father's gambling debts. Told me that he'd been successful in collecting them. That individually they didn't amount to much, but when taken together and held by one person…" She shuddered at the glee her father had displayed. "He told me that your father was on the point of losing every-thing. That if I continued to entertain your suit, he would call on your father and demand immediate payment of all the notes."

"I don't think they amounted to that much, Abigail. He had, on occasion, lost more than he should, but never so much that he'd be ruined. He wasn't that reckless."

She closed her eyes briefly, agony stabbing her again at everything she'd lost because of her father's lies. "I didn't know that. I couldn't have known. The way he described it, I feared you'd be left with nothing. I couldn't be the reason your family lost everything."

"So he insisted that you end things between us and accept Holbrook's suit instead."

"Yes. He told me that he would destroy the notes if I followed along with his wishes."

"There was no guarantee he'd do that. If my father had lost more than was wise, it was possible your father still would have demanded repayment of the debt after you married."

She let out a soft sigh. "I know. My father can be a vengeful man when he's thwarted. He would have enjoyed taking away whatever he could from your family. But on the day of my wedding, I confronted him about it. I threatened to break off the engagement with Holbrook—to do it at the cathedral if need be, in front of all our acquaintances. I demanded that he burn the notes he'd shown me. I waited and watched him do it. I knew I'd done the right thing when he refused to speak to me for the rest of the day."

Cranston was silent for a full minute.

Her shoulders drooped. "You don't believe me."

He shook his head. "On the contrary, I do. From everything I've learned recently, your story doesn't surprise me."

She tried to hold back her tears. "Perhaps we can start again…"

"I can't, Abigail. We can still continue as man and wife and be there for Gemma. Perhaps give her siblings if we're so blessed. But the life we'd both foreseen having together…" He shrugged. "I'm not that man anymore."

# CHAPTER 15

He left Abigail in the drawing room, telling her he'd ask the housekeeper to give her a tour of the house.

And after asking his butler to relay that message, he escaped to his study.

Their conversation left him feeling unsettled. He was steadfast in the knowledge that he would never again risk the pain of heartbreak, but he felt an undeniable measure of relief at knowing his judgment about Abigail all those years ago hadn't been totally wrong.

He supposed they'd both suffered. She in a loveless marriage and then banished to the countryside where she knew no one, and he when he'd entered military service.

He would have to proceed with caution. He could no longer blame her for harm that had been done to the two of them, but neither could he allow her to get too close.

Which was why he remained in his study, distracting himself by going over the reports his steward had sent him, until it was time for dinner.

When he didn't find her in the drawing room or any of the rooms on the main floor, he asked his butler to let her know he was ready for dinner.

The man coughed discreetly. "Lady Cranston made arrangements for dinner to be brought to her room."

Cranston frowned. "She won't be joining me then?" He hadn't foreseen that she might also have decided it was best to avoid him. But surely she didn't mean to hide in her bedchamber forever.

"No, my lord. She asked me to let you know you should join her there."

A thrill of anticipation surged through him. Whatever else could be said about their relationship, he very much wanted it to be a physical one. And it appeared Abigail was of the same mind.

He thanked the man and made his way to her bedchamber. When he knocked, she bade him enter.

The sun was just starting to set and candles had already been lit. A great deal of them, lending the room a cozy, warm glow. He hadn't been in this room since taking up residence last year. At the time he reasoned it was because he had no interest in marrying anytime soon. But now he realized it was because a part of him was mourning the fact that this room would never belong to Abigail.

His gaze was drawn to the small table that had been set up in one corner. Covered dishes sat on its surface as well as on the dressing table.

She'd gone to a great deal of effort to make their first night together special. Far more effort than he'd managed, and a rush of shame coursed through him at the realization that he wasn't worthy of this woman who had sacrificed her own happiness to ensure his family wasn't ruined.

His eyes swept across the room, and then he saw her standing in the doorway of her dressing room.

Clad only in a white nightdress that clung to the curves of her body.

He swallowed hard when she began to walk toward him and he realized that a large slit had been cut along the side seam of the skirt, going almost all the way up to her hip. Her entire leg was bared with every step she took.

"I wasn't sure you'd join me tonight." Her voice was soft, husky, and he could tell she was looking forward to their night together as much as he was.

He wanted to throw her onto the bed and ravish her, but it would be more enjoyable if they drew out the anticipation of what would be happening tonight. And if he was being honest with himself, he needed to get a measure of control over the lust raging through his body.

"As I told you when I proposed, there would be no point in having a wife I never meant to touch."

Her smile told him she was pleased with his reply.

He held out her chair, his eyes glued to the slit in her tempting nightdress. It wasn't until she'd sat down that his gaze moved up her body and he realized that the upper part of the dress was so sheer he could almost see right through it. The press of her hard nipples against the fabric was unmistakable.

Oh yes, she was just as aroused as he. He couldn't help but wonder if she'd touched herself while she was waiting for him to arrive.

And with that errant thought, his erection became almost painful.

He lowered his head and spoke low in her ear.

"I'm going to enjoy tearing that infernal scrap of fabric from your body." A shiver coursed through her, and he saw gooseflesh rise along her bare arms.

Good. They could both be in pain right now. It would make their pleasure all the sweeter.

He took the chair opposite. The table was small enough that he could reach out and take hold of her hand if he wanted. Instead, he watched her remove the cover from her dish, and then he did the same.

She poured a glass of wine for each of them. "Your housekeeper assured me this was one of your favorite meals."

He hadn't even looked at his plate, but he saw now that they would be having roasted pheasant. His gaze swung to the other dishes on the dressing table. "And for dessert?"

"We still have wedding cake… or me."

He growled before he realized he'd meant to make the sound.

She widened her eyes in mock innocence, and he vowed to make her beg before the evening was over.

They spoke little as they ate. He struggled not to shovel the food into his mouth so they could move on to more pleasant things. But the only thing that kept him intent on drawing the meal out as long as possible was the way she kept shifting in her chair, telling him that she was suffering just as much as him.

She pushed her plate away when it was only half-eaten and finished the rest of her wine.

He raised one brow and swirled his own drink in its cup. He wouldn't be getting foxed tonight. "Is the meal not to your liking?"

She wet her lips. "I was thinking that I would enjoy something else instead."

"Shall I fetch the cake?"

She bit her lip and shook her head.

And just like that, he gave up all pretense. He downed the rest of the wine and stood.

He extended his hand to her. When she placed her smaller one in his, he pulled her to stand.

"If you want to stop at any time—"

She placed a finger on his mouth. "I won't want to stop. I've been dreaming of this, dreaming of you, for so long."

He crushed her against him, taking a moment to enjoy the way her soft curves molded against the hard planes of his chest. Then, as if by silent accord, their mouths met in a kiss that spoke of long-denied passions.

He'd been with many women, but none could ever compare to the one in his arms. He pushed aside the significance of that realization and gave himself up to sensation.

Her fingers dug into his hair as though she were afraid he would disappear. When he cupped her backside and lifted her against his hard length, she made a soft, heated sound and wrapped her legs around his waist. He'd never been gladder for that long slit that had tormented him throughout their dinner.

He carried her to the bed but turned so he was sitting with her in his lap. Her movements against him quickened, and he realized she was going to reach her peak.

He tore his mouth from hers and buried his face in her neck so she wouldn't see how he'd gritted his teeth with the effort to keep himself from spilling in his trousers.

Finally she let out a low moan and arched her back as her entire body stiffened. Then she softened against him and he pulled her away from his aching hardness.

He reached into her hair and released the pins,

sending them scattering to the floor so he could bury his fingers in the mass of blond hair. He couldn't touch her hair the one time they'd been together since they'd both needed to return to the ball from which they'd stolen away. But he'd dreamed of how it would feel flowing over his body.

Finally, when her breathing had slowed, she pulled back to look at him. Her bottom lip was caught between her teeth, red coloring her cheeks.

He cupped her face and drew his thumb along her lower lip, freeing it. "There's to be no embarrassment here, when we're alone together like this."

When she nodded, he loosened his grip on her body. "Good. Now stand up and step out of that damned nightdress."

She gave a soft laugh. "I thought you wanted to rip it from my body?"

"I've changed my mind. I hope to see you in this—and out of it—often."

He couldn't resist weighing one of her heavy breasts in his hand and toying with the nipple.

She gasped at his boldness but then scurried off his lap. He was about to protest when she turned away from him, but then his mouth dropped open when he saw that the entire back, from her shoulders to just above the swell of her hips, was made from a sheer material that *was* transparent. He'd been so distracted by the slit in her skirt that displayed her leg that he hadn't even looked at her back when he'd helped her into her seat earlier.

"I'm infinitely glad I decided not to destroy this outfit."

She chuckled. "Amelia took me to her modiste and gave her free license to create whatever licentious designs she could imagine. I wasn't brave enough to wear one of the others."

He'd have to make a point to have John thank his wife. But for now he watched as Abigail undid a fastening at the top of the garment before allowing it to puddle at her feet.

His eyes scanned over her figure, from her long blond hair down to her slip of a waist, the curve of her hips, and her long legs.

When she stepped out of the pile of fabric and turned to face him again, her arms were crossed over her breasts. He allowed his eyes to sweep over her body, then reached forward to draw her arms down to her side.

Her breasts were larger now, the tips darker, and he wondered if the change had been caused by carrying their child. He tugged her toward him and she came willingly, stopping between his outstretched legs. He was still sitting on the edge of the bed, which put him at the perfect height to draw a breast into his mouth.

She gasped while he went about savoring his favorite dessert.

# CHAPTER 16

It was almost impossible to believe she wasn't dreaming. That she hadn't fallen asleep while waiting for Cranston to join her for dinner. But her imagination wasn't that good, and she could never have conjured all these glorious sensations in her mind.

The night she'd conceived Gemma, she'd been young and innocent. Cranston had given her pleasure, yes, but there had also been pain. He'd promised her that the next time they were together there would be only pleasure. But that day had never come.

Instead, she'd married an old man who thought only of himself during their brief couplings. Which had come as a relief because it meant they were of short duration. He'd spend himself inside her and then leave through the connecting door to his own bedchamber. Often without saying a word to her.

Those visits had continued throughout her pregnancy, but once she'd given birth, he'd sent her away. No one had touched her since. That had suited her well because she'd only wanted this man.

The wait had been well worth it.

She'd been mortified at how she'd used him for her own pleasure and had been half-afraid he would mock her for it. Perhaps use her neediness against her. But at least here, in the bedchamber, Cranston was generous with her.

His soft suckling at her breasts brought back the ache between her legs. She hadn't thought it possible to want him again so soon after achieving her release. She'd planned to see the rest of their wedding night through, to make sure he also found his pleasure, but it appeared her body was not yet finished with this man.

She looked down to find him watching her as he released her breast.

"I believe you're wearing far too much clothing, my lord."

He was grinning as he rose to his feet. "By all means, allow me to remedy the situation."

He swept his hand over the bed and she took the invitation to lie down. She longed to crawl under the bedsheets, her bravado already at its limits after stepping out of the nightdress. Amelia had assured her that men liked to watch women undress and had urged her to push aside her reservations. Still, at least now that she was reclining, she could raise her knees to shield her privates, and she draped an arm over her breasts.

Cranston's lips quirked up when he saw her belated attempts at modesty, but he didn't mock her for them. Instead, he proceeded to step out of his clothing.

When he was down to just his lawn shirt, which hung down to midthigh, she bit her lip, wondering if he was going to remove that as well. She'd never seen a man totally nude before. Her one time with Cranston had been a hurried celebration when she'd accepted his marriage proposal, and her late husband had always worn a nightshirt when they were together.

Cranston stared into her eyes for several seconds and then with a quick movement drew the shirt over his head. He stood proud, no hint of embarrassment on his face, and she could certainly see why.

He was more beautiful than any man had a right to be. When he was younger, he hadn't been quite so broad across the shoulders, and now she could see that it was because he'd gained a good deal of muscle during his time of military service.

Her eyes trailed downward, noting the muscle definition of his abdomen, which was far different than her own flat stomach. But even more shocking —and thrilling—was the long, hard length of him that stood proudly, making his desire for her known.

"Do I meet with your approval?"

Embarrassed, she tore her gaze away from his body. She hadn't meant to stare for quite so long. She wasn't sure what she expected to see in his eyes. Mockery? Teasing? There had been a light tone to the words, but his eyes were filled with a heat that had her foolish heart turning over in her chest. And heavens, how his undisguised desire filled her with desperate need for him.

She was incapable of speech, so instead she held a hand out to him, the movement baring her breasts to his gaze again. She wasn't brave enough to lower her knee until he took hold of that hand and joined her on the bed.

He braced himself over her on his elbows and stared down at her. The moment stretched, taut with the promise of what would happen next. It was more intense than anything she'd ever experienced. She'd thought their first time together had been special, if a bit rushed, but this night eclipsed that encounter.

Unable to speak, she reached up to wrap her arms around him again, drawing his head down to hers. He lowered himself over her then, and the shock of feeling his skin pressing against hers everywhere was almost too much to bear.

There was no softness in his kiss, and he used one hand to trace his way down her body, stopping to squeeze both her breasts and tease her nipples before continuing further.

She gasped into his mouth when he touched her between her legs, but he didn't stop kissing her. He swirled a thumb over the bundle of nerves that rested just above her opening, the way he had done all those years ago when he'd prepared her for their first joining. Her late husband had never bothered to touch her there, caring only for his own pleasure before leaving. But Cranston… She let out a soft moan when he entered her with two fingers and began to mimic the act of lovemaking with his hand.

He raised his head to watch her, but she was beyond embarrassment. When he dipped his head to take a breast into his mouth again, that was all it took for release to sweep over her.

Twice. He'd given her pleasure twice before even thinking about himself. But he was doing that now. He lifted her leg over his back, and she did the same with the other as he finally entered her.

There was no shock of pain with him this time. And her late husband's inept fumblings were driven from her mind as Cranston plundered her body. Gone was the finesse he'd been showing, but she found that she didn't care. His hard strokes had her, impossibly, climbing higher than she'd thought possible.

He was panting into her ear as he moved within her, his body strong and confident, and she let out a wanton moan with each powerful thrust.

He raised his head to stare down at her again, and their gazes locked. "I need you to come for me again, Abigail." His thrusts moved even deeper, a little slower. The drag of his body over that bundle of nerves, the feel of his hard cock filling her… She was powerless to resist the command.

Her body tightened again, and she let out a cry of surprise.

His thrusts became erratic as her channel tightened over him, and then with a groan, he stiffened deep within her and emptied himself.

He stayed frozen over her for some time, his weight pushing her into her feather mattress, before pulling out and rolling onto his back. Abigail turned her head to look at him, but his gaze was fixed on the ceiling.

She wanted to say something. To let him know that this experience had surpassed anything she'd ever imagined. But something had shifted in the air between them, and she couldn't say what caused her to hold back the words.

Finally he turned to look at her. His expression had been wiped clean of all passion, and a swooping sense of dread settled in her belly.

She could only watch as he sat up, then stood. He bent to pick up his pile of clothing and then, without looking back at her, strode from the room.

She couldn't help feeling that she had done something wrong. Had she been too wanton? She could have sworn he'd enjoyed wringing pleasure from her.

She shifted until she could get under the

bedsheets. Her wedding night had shattered her expectations. And now the realization that this was just another coupling for him—no different than what he'd shared with a number of other women if rumors were to be believed—threatened to shatter her heart.

# CHAPTER 17

Their wedding night had gone much better than he could have expected.

Cranston grimaced at the tepid description for what had passed between him and Abigail. The consummation of their marriage had been incendiary. It threatened to tear away the walls he'd erected around his heart, forming undeniable cracks.

He wasn't ready. Not yet. He'd been angry with Abigail for too many years. Had convinced himself that all women were fickle.

It pained him to realize he wasn't quite as jaded as he'd believed. Which meant his heart was in danger, and that thought terrified him. There was nothing for it but to keep his distance from Abigail.

For now at least. He couldn't just fall under her spell again. He wouldn't.

But he had no problem letting Gemma into his heart. Hell, she'd smashed her way into it after their introduction.

When she arrived that morning, she burst into the house like a small hurricane, a doll clutched in her hands. Her governess trailed behind her, shaking her head in exasperation at her charge's exuberance.

Abigail gathered her up in her arms and gave her a tight squeeze. "I missed you this morning."

Gemma's arms wrapped around her mother's neck. "It was strange not having breakfast with you."

Abigail released her, and Gemma looked up at him, shy for the first time since he'd met her.

He crouched. "We can all have breakfast together now."

A smile lit her face, and she took the two steps that separated them and gave him a quick hug. He wanted to clutch her to him as Abigail had done, but it was too soon for that. He'd have to let her lead when it came to their relationship. She might have accepted him as her father, but it would still take time for her to grow completely comfortable around him.

"Let me show you around the house. Your room is ready for you."

It was easy to avoid Abigail while not going out of his way to make it look like he was avoiding her with Gemma there. Her lessons were suspended for the day since his daughter wouldn't have been able to concentrate on anything other than the way her life had completely changed.

He knew it wasn't customary, but they had dinner together *en famille*. He couldn't recall ever doing so at her age, He'd always eaten in the nursery with his nurse and then his tutor when he was older. After that, he'd gone away to school. He was quite a bit older when it was deemed appropriate for him to join his parents for the evening meal.

But he enjoyed himself more than he'd thought he would. He couldn't remember the last time he'd used this room but now he could foresee making their family dinner a daily ritual.

After the meal, they retired to the drawing room, and Gemma asked him to tell her a story from his years in the army. He hated to think about that time. There were so many things he'd seen and done that he never wanted to relive. His nightmares wouldn't allow him to escape them, but he wouldn't share that part of his experiences with Gemma.

Instead, he told her about some of the amusing antics that the men in his regiment would get up to during the quiet times. Some of those men were gone now, their lives snuffed out in service to their country. But he wanted to remember them in those quiet, happy moments, and it gave him joy to share those stories.

At some point Gemma leaned against him and he wrapped an arm around her, drawing her closer to his side. It wasn't long before he noticed that her eyes were starting to droop.

He tweaked her nose. "I think I'll continue this tomorrow." He looked at Abigail. "If I'm not mistaken, I think it might be time for you to go to bed now."

Abigail nodded, smiling at the two of them. That smile did something funny to his chest, and he had to look away lest he fall under the woman's spell again tonight.

Gemma pouted. "I want to hear the rest of the story. What happened when the soldier fell into the river?"

He chuckled at the way she opened her eyes a

little wider than normal, intent on convincing him that she wasn't about to fall asleep.

"Tomorrow night, my gem." He stood and held his hand out to her.

She scrunched her nose, and for a moment he feared she was going to protest the way he'd shortened her name. She didn't take his hand when she stood, going to her mother instead.

Abigail engulfed her in a hug. "Sweet dreams, Gemma."

"Good night, Mama," she said, placing a kiss on her mother's cheek.

He'd allowed his hand to drop to his side, disappointed. But instead of him having to watch while Abigail took her upstairs, Gemma came to his side and slipped her hand into his.

To her credit, Abigail stayed back as he brought their daughter upstairs. Gemma was already so mature. He didn't think there would be many more opportunities to do this with her. Before long, she'd be rolling her eyes at him and telling him that she was old enough to go upstairs on her own.

Miss Phillips heard them coming and came out of her own room, which was next to Gemma's.

"Good night, Papa," she said, giving him a quick hug before going into her bedchamber.

He murmured a quiet "good night" to her and nodded to the governess.

When the door closed behind them, he remained standing in the hallway. He could hear their voices through the wood door, but that wasn't the reason he stayed.

He didn't know what to do now. He knew what he *wanted* to do. He wanted to go downstairs, get Abigail, and bring her back to his bedchamber so they could indulge in another bout of vigorous lovemaking.

His blood heated at the memories of how glorious and giving she'd been last night. And with those memories, his cock hardened.

He swore under his breath and headed for his study. He needed distance. When he had this overwhelming need to sate himself within this woman under control, he would go to her again. They could try to conceive another child, give Gemma a brother or a sister. She would like that.

And if he was being honest with himself, so would he.

# CHAPTER 18

*D*espite the way Cranston had left her on their wedding night, Abigail held on to the belief that their marriage would be different than her first. That Cranston would come to see her as more than someone with whom to satisfy his physical needs.

But in the three weeks since their wedding night, he'd only come to her bed three more times. Despite the fact that they broke their fast and had dinner together as a family each day, the gulf between them was still there.

She was beginning to fear it would always be this way. She wanted so much more, but if this was all she could have with Cranston, she would take it and cherish each brief moment together.

For those moments *were* brief. After making love —and heavens, the man was thorough when it came to lovemaking—he would get up and leave.

And each time that happened, she had to force herself not to beg him to stay.

This was how marriage was conducted within the *ton*. She knew that Amelia and her husband shared a bed, and she imagined that Mary and her new husband Lord Ashford would as well. But it was clear that such an arrangement wasn't in her future.

At least Cranston wouldn't be banishing her to a far-off estate.

After breakfast that morning, Gemma went upstairs to begin her lessons for the day. When Cranston took his leave shortly thereafter, as he did every morning, she watched him go with a sigh.

She'd just finished meeting with the house-keeper, a lovely older woman who'd been thrilled that the baron had finally settled down, when a footman presented her with a note.

She smiled when she recognized Amelia's hand-writing.

*I wanted to let you know that I'll be calling later*
*this morning.*

*And I have a surprise for you.*

*(Gird your loins.)*

*—Amelia*

She shook her head at the dramatics, wondering what the marchioness had planned. Perhaps another shopping trip. She hadn't had a chance yet to wear all the nightdresses they'd purchased the last time.

Well, that wasn't strictly true. She'd worn them, yes, but Cranston had only seen her in two of them. She had five of the scandalous garments, each one more shocking than the last. She donned one each night, hoping that her husband would visit her bedchamber. They'd made love four times—yes, she was counting—but he'd only seen two of the night-dresses. His eyes had lit with delight when he'd seen the second one, made of deep blue satin. If he'd bothered to visit her more often, he would have been shocked at some of the ones he hadn't yet seen.

It struck her then that perhaps Amelia would be announcing that she and Lowenbrock were finally going to leave town.

She felt a pang of sorrow, but it was to be expected. Amelia had told her that she was no longer feeling unwell every morning. No doubt she was anxious to return to the house where she'd been raised.

Abigail settled into the drawing room with her embroidery. As her fingers moved over the small cushion cover she was working on, she had to force her thoughts to stop drifting back to her husband. He'd visited her bed two nights ago, so she knew it would be several days before he came to her again.

She spent the next hour in that manner, her fingers moving over the flower pattern she was following and giving in to her daydreams about a future where she and Cranston had finally overcome their difficulties and were as happy together as her friends were in their marriages.

When a knock sounded at the front door, she set her needlework into the small basket on the table next to her and rose to her feet.

She smiled when Amelia stepped into the doorway, then let out a soft cry of astonishment when she was followed into the room by the new Viscountess Ashford.

She rushed forward to hug the woman, shocked

to find Mary was actually standing in her drawing room.

"You were holding back on us," Mary said when she pulled back. "I can't believe you went and married Cranston the moment we left town! Were the two of you having a secret love affair behind our backs?"

Abigail couldn't hold back an indelicate snort. "If only that were true. Come in and sit down. Refreshments will be served shortly."

The staff knew that they were to bring in a few chocolate sweets whenever Amelia visited. She would have to learn what Mary favored before her next visit.

"I feared you were calling to tell me that you were quitting London," she said as they lowered themselves onto the settee. She took the seat at one end so she could look at both women.

Amelia grimaced. "John and I have been talking about it. But now that Mary and Ashford have returned from their wedding trip, I'm sure we'll be putting it off again."

"Where did you go? Tell us all about it," Abigail said. She would never have a wedding trip of her own and so would have to live vicariously through the viscountess.

Mary let out a wistful sigh. "It was delightful. We went to Brighton to enjoy the sea air. Ashford rented a small cottage there, but in the end we spent *a great deal of time* inside. We'll need to go back at some point to take in the sights that we missed."

Amelia laughed and placed a hand on the slight swell of her belly. "I wonder how long it will be before this one here has a playmate when we're all in London together."

Mary shook her head. "Given my husband's virility, I doubt it will be long."

Although Abigail was happy for her friends, she couldn't help but feel a small pang of jealousy. She yearned for that type of relationship with her husband even though she knew it to be a foolish wish.

Mary turned to her then, her arms crossed. "Don't think to distract me with your questions. I'll answer them all later, but first it is your turn. To say that I was shocked when I received Amelia's letter with the news that the two of you had wed would be a vast understatement." There was a slight frown on the woman's face, but Abigail could tell Mary wasn't truly angry.

Abigail opened her mouth to reply but stilled when she heard the soft footfall of her husband's tread coming down the hallway. No doubt the staff had informed him of her guests' visit and he was coming to see for himself.

"Cranston is coming," she said, her voice low.

Her husband stepped into the room and groaned when his eyes landed on Mary. "I thought the staff was mistaken when they told me you were here."

Mary scowled at him. "You wretch. You could have waited for us to return before running off and getting married yourself."

Cranston raised a brow. "It's not 'running off' if I remained in London." At Mary's huff of annoyance, he chuckled. "I thought you and Ashford were going to his estate after leaving Brighton."

Their refreshments were brought in then, and Abigail set about pouring everyone's tea while she watched the viscountess spar verbally with Cranston.

"That was the plan. Then he received word that his mother had quit town and was looking forward to seeing the two of us in Suffolk. He'd been under the mistaken impression she was planning to visit his youngest sister after leaving town since she is with child, but apparently there are still a few months before her confinement. The dowager viscountess won't be visiting until the time draws nearer."

Cranston nodded. "I can understand why he'd change plans. His mother was quite… *intense*… during the wedding preparations. I'm sure he isn't up for that level of scrutiny anytime soon."

Amelia shook her head. "So instead, the two of you decided to return to London and subject yourselves to our scrutiny?"

Mary lifted one shoulder in a casual shrug. "It's not scrutiny when one is among friends."

"It's support," Abigail said.

Mary nodded. "Yes, exactly."

Cranston shook his head. "Well, the three of you should try not to get into any trouble while I'm gone. I imagine your husbands are at White's?" At Mary's nod, he continued. "Then I suppose I should get the upcoming ordeal over with quickly. I can already hear Ashford's scolding." He raised his eyes to the heavens as though offering up a silent prayer for strength and then took his leave.

They watched him go. Mary held her hands in her lap and waited. Abigail knew what would happen as soon as they heard the sound of the front door closing behind him.

"Tell me *everything*," Mary exclaimed, leaning

forward with a gleam in her eyes that told Abigail she wouldn't be distracted a second time. "Amelia wouldn't tell me what happened. When we got the letter that the two of you had wed..." She shook her head. "I still can't believe it. I half expected that Amelia was bringing me here just to laugh at me and tell me she was trying to see just how gullible I was."

Abigail met Amelia's gaze. "You didn't tell her?"

Amelia shook her head. "It's not my tale to tell."

"You see?" Mary said, throwing her hands up in the air. "She's positively infuriating. I'd hoped that the two of you could rekindle your past romance, but I never expected it to happen so quickly."

Abigail sighed. "I hate to disappoint you, but that still hasn't happened." She blushed as she thought about their heated lovemaking sessions.

Mary frowned. "Then why did you get married?"

Abigail took a deep breath before answering. "You know I have a daughter?" At Mary's nod, she continued. "Cranston is her father."

Mary sucked in her breath, her eyes widening with shock. "How..." She shook her head. "Never mind, I know how. I don't want to assume the worst about either of you, so I'll reserve judgment until you tell me everything."

Abigail couldn't blame the woman. At least Mary was giving her the chance to explain. "We were only together once. It was just before my father forced me to accept another's suit. And when I told Cranston I was marrying someone else…" Her voice hitched.

"He purchased a commission and left London," Amelia finished for her.

Mary shook her head. "So he never knew, and neither did you before you were married?"

Abigail shook her head. "Father insisted on a special license. I think he was afraid that I'd elope with Cranston. But that wasn't going to happen because Father had convinced me that he had the power to ruin Cranston's family."

Mary wrapped an arm around her. "That's horrible."

"The look on his face when I told him…" She shook her head, trying to push back the memory. She wouldn't cry.

"That man doesn't hate you," Mary said. "Does he know what happened?"

"Yes," she said with a sigh. "But it doesn't

matter. He says he's changed and that he can't love me again."

Amelia reached across Mary to put a reassuring hand on her knee.

"I've come to terms with it," Abigail said. "It's enough that he's here for Gemma. You'll see for yourself. He's so good with her, and Gemma adores him."

Mary met Amelia's gaze, and something unspoken passed between them.

"I can almost hear the wheels turning in that brain of yours," Amelia said.

Mary grinned. "You know me too well. I do have an idea."

Abigail shook her head. "It's enough that we're married. We can't make him fall in love with me."

Mary's head tilted to one side. "And what if he's still in love with you? Heaven knows that man has been with a number of women in the short time I've known him, but never with the same one twice. And he chose to marry you."

"Because he wanted to be close to Gemma."

Mary's eyes narrowed. "He has connections. He could have forced the issue. Made arrangements to take custody of her for himself."

Abigail had feared just that outcome, but she'd

refused to believe the man she'd known all those years ago could be that cruel. That he could have changed that much.

"He would never do that."

"Perhaps not, but he could have contented himself with staying detached. Many men have bastards, after all. And most don't feel the need to wed the mother of their children."

Abigail agreed, which was why she'd been shocked when he proposed. "I never expected him to want to marry me just so he could be closer to Gemma."

"And you," Mary said. "He might have used Gemma as the excuse, but he also gained you. The only woman he's ever wanted to wed."

Abigail shook her head. "I don't think that was his reasoning. I think he was just trying to make the best of an unpleasant situation."

"Perhaps we can press the issue. Entice him to reveal his true feelings."

Amelia was silent during their exchange, but now she frowned. "I'm not sure that's wise. We've interfered enough."

Mary sighed. "You mean *I've* interfered enough."

"Your heart was in the right place when you

invited Abigail to your wedding breakfast."

Abigail felt the blood drain from her face. "That wasn't a happy accident?" She straightened her shoulders and faced the woman, asking the question she didn't really want to know the answer to. "How much did Cranston tell you about me? Or was it Ashford who told you?"

Mary sighed. "It was Ashford, of course. But it wasn't like that. It wasn't idle gossip about your husband's past."

She wouldn't assume the worst. If Cranston could sit and allow her to explain what had happened all those years ago, she could do the same for these two women she considered friends.

"I'm listening. But first... Is this friendship a ruse?" She winced slightly, hating how the question made her feel needy. "A way to help Cranston find his own happy ending?"

Mary took hold of both of Abigail's hands and squeezed them. "No, it's not like that. Not entirely."

Amelia frowned. "If you're trying to reassure her, you're doing a terrible job."

Mary huffed. "I'm not the one who's good with words. Let me try again. Do you remember that first day when Amelia and I met you?"

Abigail nodded. "I'd just arrived in town and

was visiting the shops on Bond Street, looking for a few items we needed at the house. You were kind enough to point out some of your favorite shops."

"Yes, that's right. Amelia and I decided after that first meeting that we wanted to get to know you better."

Amelia nodded. "That's true. We're so used to scheming women who only care about advancing themselves. You didn't even ask us about our husbands, which is rare. It meant that you cared more about us as people and not just about how you could use a connection with us to advance yourself."

Abigail could concede that point. "I've noticed that myself. But since I hadn't been happily married and tried not to think about my own marriage…" She lifted one shoulder in a shrug. "Discussing husbands has never been something I enjoyed doing."

"Well, shortly after, Ashford and I were at Hyde Park during the fashionable hour. We met Cranston there and walked together for a little bit. I spotted you and mentioned that we'd met and that Amelia and I wanted to become better acquainted with you."

Abigail could just imagine how Cranston had taken that news. "I didn't see you."

"Yes, well, Cranston had this strange look on his face and froze in place. I assumed that meant he'd already dallied with you since I knew you were a widow."

Abigail tried not to reveal how much she hated the idea that her husband might very well have slept with every widow in London in the one year since he'd returned from war.

"Ashford hastened me away."

"So he knew."

"I heard him ask your husband if you were 'the one.' Then when we left, he told me that Cranston had been in love once and had his heart broken."

Abigail had to look away, shame overtaking her.

"That was all we knew," Amelia added.

"I don't think our husbands knew more than that. And until that day, they didn't even know who the woman in question was," Mary said.

Amelia nodded. "We don't blame you. We all know that women don't always get to choose whom they wed."

Abigail shook her head. "Well, you can rest assured that I did *not* want to marry someone who was older than my father, especially not when I was in love with someone else."

Amelia's face softened with sympathy. "With Cranston."

"Yes."

"I didn't know how he felt about you. No one ever mentioned the matter after that. Ashford was just trying to warn me that perhaps it would be better if I didn't pursue a friendship with you."

Abigail smiled. "Well, I for one am glad you ignored him. But you should know that I always meant to tell Cranston the truth. Your invitation just provided me with a convenient way to approach him."

"And it has all worked out," Amelia said.

Mary shook her head. "We need to test him."

Abigail didn't like the sound of that. "Please tell me what you're planning. I don't like the idea of tricking my husband."

"Oh no, never that. I just thought that now that we're back in town, we should host a party. Perhaps a small ball?"

Amelia balked at that. "Only if you're the one planning to host it. Besides, there aren't many people still here. Mostly bachelors."

"But there are a few?" Mary asked.

Abigail nodded. "Yes. Mostly…"

Her voice trailed off. Mostly widows.

"We can host a dinner party then. It doesn't need to be anything as formal as a ball. And you"—Mary looked directly at her—"can flirt with some of those bachelors."

Abigail cringed. "Absolutely not."

Mary sighed. "Or you could just allow them to flirt with you. Then we can see if your husband becomes jealous."

"No. I want him to trust me. I've already hurt him in the past and married someone else. Why on earth would I betray his trust again?" Abigail shook her head. "The first time I was young and my father forced my hand. But this time I would have no excuse."

Mary slumped back against the cushions of the settee.

"Widows," Amelia said.

Abigail looked away.

"What do you mean?" Mary asked.

"The majority of people still in town are bachelors and widows. Women who are enjoying their freedom now that their husbands have passed away. They don't want to stay buried in the country."

Mary smiled. "We can see how Cranston

behaves with these other women. If he shows any indication of wanting to bed one of them…"

Mary's voice trailed off when she looked at Abigail.

She knew what the woman was seeing. Abigail felt as though she were going to be ill. The thought of having to witness her husband flirting with another woman. She closed her eyes to hold back a grimace of pain.

Amelia sighed. "I think it's a good idea."

"And how would you feel if it were your husbands we were throwing at women who wanted to bed them?" Her tone was harsher than she'd intended, but she didn't want to do this.

"Abigail." Mary's tone was sympathetic. "That happens every time we are out in society. It doesn't matter how innocuous the event. There's always at least one woman who wants to lure them away."

Amelia nodded. "I foolishly thought that behavior would stop after we married, but it didn't. It just changed from young women who hoped to ensnare them as husbands to widows and other married women who just want a quick tumble."

Abigail blew out a breath. If what her friends were saying was correct—and why would they lie about such a thing?—then this was something she would soon face herself, with or without their schemes.

Perhaps it was better to get this first trial over with quickly. If Cranston planned to be unfaithful, it might be better for her heart to come to terms with that fact as soon as possible.

She hated the cold-bloodedness of this "test" that her friends were proposing, but there was no point in delaying the inevitable.

"What did you have in mind?"

# CHAPTER 19

They settled on a small house party to be held at the Lowenbrock town house in one week's time. Amelia grumbled about it, but Mary had recently undergone the ordeal of planning her wedding with a mother-in-law who'd been just a little overbearing in her enthusiasm. And neither of her friends thought it appropriate for Abigail to host the house party that could very well lead to her heartbreak.

There would be no formal dinner, no dancing, just people enjoying an evening of chatter and light refreshments. The music room would also be kept open if anyone wanted to sit down at the pianoforte, but guests wouldn't be expected to gather round as they would had Amelia been hosting a more formal musicale.

Abigail's emotions had her going back and forth several times about the wisdom of attending the event. When the day of the party finally arrived, she almost told Cranston that she had a headache and needed to stay home. She'd been plagued with them of late, so he might believe her.

She didn't need to be there tonight. Her friends could let her know what happened. How he behaved with other women. If it appeared as though he was considering taking one as a lover. But Abigail forced herself to face this first test of what their future together would be like.

So now she was standing with Amelia and Mary in the salon near the back of the Lowenbrock town house. It was early evening and candles lit the large room. Doors opened onto the garden, which allowed a pleasant evening breeze to cool the crowded room.

Abigail's friends chatted with her, pretending that they couldn't tell she was watching her husband flitter from guest to guest. She was particularly interested in his interactions with the women.

She hated the way their gazes followed Cranston hungrily, as though he were a morsel to be enjoyed at their leisure. While it was true that they did the same with Mary's and Amelia's husbands, it was a million times worse with Cranston. Everyone could see that their attempts to lure Ashford and Lowenbrock away were futile because the men were clearly in love with their wives. But it was equally clear that her husband… wasn't.

Lord Holbrook approached and handed her a cup of ratafia. "Excuse my presumption, but I thought you'd like a refreshment."

She smiled at the viscount as she accepted the cup. Holbrook was always dressed well, but he looked particularly handsome tonight in his dark blue coat and gold breeches. He'd attracted no small amount of attention himself.

She noticed the way her friends melted away, leaving her alone with the man.

She smiled at him, grateful for his attentiveness to her, and took a sip of the drink. "You've been too kind to me."

He shrugged. "It's a pity there's no dancing tonight. It occurs to me that we could try our hand at trying to make your husband jealous instead of it being the other way around."

She hadn't realized until that moment that he'd

angled his body away and that she'd followed the movement unconsciously. She could no longer see Cranston from this angle, and it would be too embarrassing to shift her position now so she could watch what he was doing.

"It would be a futile effort." She let out a soft breath, hating how observant Holbrook was. Worse, she realized that everyone in the room might be feeling pity for her.

He leaned down so he was closer. "He's watching us, and I can assure you that he's most displeased."

She looked up at Holbrook, wondering why he seemed to take pleasure in trying to provoke her husband. But she'd already told her friends that she wouldn't play this game and risk losing her husband's trust again.

"I appreciate your concern, but I can assure you all is well between us."

He offered her his arm. "Would you take a turn about the room with me?"

She considered rejecting his offer but decided that it would be innocent enough. This man had walked her down the aisle at their wedding. Surely her husband wouldn't think he had anything but honest intentions toward her.

And truth be told, she was becoming increasingly annoyed with the way Cranston had been going out of his way to avoid her all evening. Why shouldn't she spend time with someone she considered a friend?

She took another sip of her drink before handing it to a passing footman. Then she slipped her hand into Holbrook's arm. "I hope you're not still in town because of me. I appreciate the way you've been looking out for me and Gemma, but you don't need to continue to put off your plans."

He shrugged. "I don't have family waiting for me there. I was heading to the Holbrook country seat to meet with the steward and familiarize myself with the property."

She looked up at him, surprised. "You haven't visited yet?"

He shook his head. "No, but I've been in contact with the steward. He seems a capable enough fellow. And my solicitor assures me the estate is well run, so there's no pressing need for me to hurry back."

"It occurs to me that I've never asked about your family."

"They're a bunch of ruffians," he said with a grimace. "I have three younger brothers, and

Mother can barely control them when they're home from school. I fear the hell they'll unleash in town when they're old enough to come down."

"They could always join you now."

"Shh," he said, looking around with exaggerated dismay. He leaned closer. "I told Mother that the town house is a shambles and in need of repair and that I've been staying at a hotel."

"You didn't!" she said with a laugh. "You're incorrigible."

They'd done their circuit around the large salon and were approaching her friends again.

"Well, I've done what I can," he said with a slight bow over her hand, and she couldn't help but notice the way he held her gaze for several seconds longer than strictly necessary. "I'll leave you now in capable hands lest your husband decide to storm over here and call me out."

She could only shake her head at the absurdity of his words as she watched him saunter away with a spring in his step.

"That was brilliant!" Mary said as she took her arm.

Amelia beamed at her. "Your husband wasn't happy that another man was paying attention to you."

Abigail let out a soft huff. "He knows where I am if he wants my company. Where is he now?"

"He's—" Mary's voice faltered as she looked over Abigail's shoulder and her smile disappeared.

Abigail no longer cared if she was being obvious. She turned to look behind her and found Cranston in a tête-à-tête with a very attractive widow who was hanging on to her husband's arm.

Ice slithered through her veins, and she feared she was going to be ill. She thought she'd prepared herself to face this possibility, but she'd been lying to herself.

"If you'll excuse me, I think I need a little air," she said to the two women. She hated the twin looks of dismay on their faces, which was further proof that she wasn't misreading the situation.

She headed to the garden doors that had been closed at some point in the evening. She realized why when she slipped through the doors and felt the light mist of rain fall on her skin.

She didn't care that it was starting to dampen her gown, she just needed to get as far away as she could from the sight of her husband with another woman.

She began to head down the path that led to the back of the garden. Mary had told her once that the Lowenbrocks had a hidden gazebo there. If she could find it, she might get some relief from the rain that was no longer just a light mist.

After several minutes of her wandering around, a hand grasped her arm. A scream rose in her throat, but she held it back and turned to give whoever had grabbed her a setdown. She sagged with relief when she saw it was Cranston.

"What are you doing here?" He gave her a quelling look and began to lead her back to the house.

She tried, but failed, to pull away from his gasp. "I can't go back inside. I'm indecent."

His eyes drifted down to the décolletage of her pale blue dress, and a muscle tensed in his jaw. With a stiff nod, he led her in the other direction.

Straight to the gazebo, which was hidden behind a small gap in the shrubs she'd just walked past.

It was very picturesque, painted white with stone benches that lined the interior, but the only thing she could think about was Cranston as he dragged her under the roof. His coat protected him from the worst of the rain, but his damp hair was hanging straight.

She ignored the urge to brush it back. The rain

had seeped into her clothing and she was beginning to feel cold, but she concentrated instead on the anger that was beginning to swell within her. He had the nerve to look at her as though she'd done something wrong when he was the one who'd been flirting with that woman who was all but falling out of her gown?

When he stopped, she pulled her arm out of his grasp and turned to glare at him. "As you can see, I'm quite well. And if you came to make sure I wasn't having an assignation, I can assure you that nothing of the sort will occur."

Why was the man just staring at her like that?

She let out a huff of annoyance. "You can go back to your lover… or soon-to-be-lover… or whatever she is to you."

She turned away, angry with him, yes, but even angrier with herself that she was letting him get under her skin like this.

"I'm not going to leave you here, Abigail."

She let out a mirthless laugh and turned to glare at him. "No, of course not. You've spent the evening flirting with every available—and unavailable—woman here, yet *I'm* the one who can't be trusted."

She would not stamp her foot or strike him, but

dear heavens how she wanted to. More than she cared to admit.

He lowered himself onto one of the benches that lined the interior of the gazebo. What was the man waiting for?

She scowled at him. "If you don't hurry, she might find someone else to warm her bed tonight."

His mouth widened in a smile that had her fingers itching to slap him.

"Why, Lady Cranston, I do believe you're jealous."

She crossed her arms under her breasts and glared at him.

HE SHOULDN'T BE ENJOYING THIS AS MUCH AS he was.

When he'd seen her slip out into the gardens, he'd thought the worst. That she was going out to meet with Holbrook since the man was suddenly nowhere to be found.

So he'd excused himself from the woman who was becoming a nuisance and followed her. He trailed behind her for a little while, making sure to keep his distance. But when it became clear that no one was waiting for her, and when the rain began to come down harder and she continued wandering through the garden, he'd made his presence known.

His eyes dipped to her bodice again. The neckline wasn't scandalous, but the way she'd unconsciously pushed up her breasts had him remembering the delicious evenings they'd spent together. They hadn't made love often enough for his liking.

He'd hoped that tonight he'd feel a stirring of desire for another woman. He had no intention of taking a lover, but it would have been evidence that he wasn't falling under Abigail's spell. Again.

But that hadn't happened. In fact, he'd been in the process of turning down one such offer of a quick tumble when he'd spied Abigail slipping out through the garden doors. All he'd cared about in that moment was making sure that she never escaped him again. He'd cared not a whit for the buxom brunette who'd been pressing her ample bounty against his arm.

Of course Abigail had noticed, and apparently she hadn't been pleased.

"So here we are, all alone in this gazebo." He

lowered his voice. "I've heard that Lowenbrock, as well as Ashford, have enjoyed the privacy provided by the high hedges that hide us from prying eyes."

Her mouth dropped open in shock when she realized what he was saying. He found it impossible to ignore the thrum of desire that began to shimmer through his veins. "Perhaps we should join that elite club."

She was silent for several seconds. "I… You… There are people…" She pressed her lips together and glared at him. "You are a horrible tease. Did I ruin your plans to meet your strumpet here?"

He was on his feet in a flash. He reached for her upper arms and yanked her against his chest. "Make no mistake, Abigail. I have no need of anyone else when you are more than enough to satisfy me."

He lowered one hand to her backside and pressed her against his rock-hard erection.

Heat flared in her eyes. He was a hairbreadth away from taking her right now, the threat of discovery be damned, when he saw her shiver.

It was only then that he realized gooseflesh rose on her arms. His eyes narrowed on her mouth, and he saw that her lips had a bluish tinge.

With a curse, he stripped off his tailcoat and wrapped it around her. "We're leaving. I need to get you home and warm you up."

# CHAPTER 20

*I* *need to get you home and warm you up.*

The memory of those words had danced along her nerve endings during the carriage ride home. He'd kept her pressed against his side, and she was grateful for his warmth. She'd been so upset she'd barely registered just how wet her dress had become. And she didn't want to imagine how unflattering her hair must look.

Cranston could have sent her home and stayed out, but instead he'd come with her. And she'd believed him when he'd said that he had no use for other women.

After settling into the hot bath her husband had ordered for her, she'd donned a demure nightdress and dismissed her maid. As soon as the woman was gone, she'd changed into the most scandalous of the nightdresses Madame Argent had created—red satin fabric that couldn't really be classified as a piece of clothing. It was a miracle that it stayed on, which was why she wore a dressing gown over it. Cranston would get a special surprise when she removed it.

Then she settled onto her bed to wait for her husband to join her and make good on his promise.

She didn't realize she was drifting off to sleep until the sound of swearing woke her.

Shouts were coming from the adjoining bedchamber. It took her sleep-dulled senses almost a full minute to understand what she was hearing. Cranston was shouting.

Her heart racing, she sat up in bed. Was someone in there with him?

She listened but could only hear one voice. His.

Which meant that he must be having a nightmare. She'd heard other women talking about how their husbands who'd returned from military service were plagued with them. Cranston hadn't told her that he suffered from the same affliction, and she hadn't thought to ask him.

She rose from the bed and walked to the adjoining door, tightening the belt of her dressing gown along the way. She hesitated when she realized he was no longer shouting. She was about to return to bed, not wanting to wake him if the nightmare had ended, when she heard another moan.

She opened the door without another thought. She couldn't take away the unpleasant memories of everything her husband had seen and done during his years in the army, but she could at least put a stop to whatever was tormenting him now.

Cranston was sprawled across the bed on his back, the bedsheets a tangle about his waist and the sheen of sweat covering his bare torso. He was muttering unintelligible words now, his brows drawn together in a fierce scowl. His hands were twitching on top of the sheets.

Anxious to help him, she rushed to the side of the bed and placed a hand on his shoulder.

"Cranston," she said as she shook him. When nothing happened, she shook him harder. "You're dreaming. You need to wake up."

She was leaning over him when his eyes sprang open. Before she could reassure him that he was only dreaming and that everything was fine, he yanked her down onto the bed and rolled them so that her body was under him.

She froze, realizing her mistake. He thought her one of the enemies he'd been battling.

"Gideon, it's me. Abigail."

He stared down at her, confusion clouding his eyes. But she saw the moment he realized who she was. He flung himself away from her, moving to sit on the edge of the bed.

"I was dreaming."

She rose and moved to sit next to him. "Yes. I heard you shouting and came in to wake you up."

He shot her a sideways look she was unable to read. "You're not afraid of me?"

"What? No, of course not. Why would I be afraid of you?"

He shook his head and looked away. It took her a few moments to realize what he wasn't saying. "This has happened with other women. You've had nightmares when…" When he slept with them. Her husband hadn't been a monk, and she wondered how many other women knew about his nightmares.

She was a fool. He didn't need her. She was just another in a long line of women who'd been intimate with him. Who'd seen him like this. She wasn't special in any way.

"Since you seem to be well now, I'll leave you."

She stood but had only managed one step when he took hold of her hand. She remained in place, refusing to look back at him.

"After the first time it happened, I never spent the entire night with another woman. She looked at me as though I were a monster who was about to commit murder."

Abigail turned to face him.

"Perhaps I am a monster now. The things I've done…" He shook his head. Then he stared into her eyes. An eternity seemed to pass before he spoke again. "But you're not afraid."

She let out a frustrated breath. "Of course I'm not afraid of you. Heaven knows I've given you plenty of reasons to hate me, but instead you've been kind. And I've seen how you are with Gemma." He still held on to one hand, and so she threaded the fingers of her other hand through his sweat dampened hair. "You could never be a monster."

His eyes searched hers, and she waited to see what he would do. Would he send her away?

"Abigail." Her name on his lips was almost a plea. "Spend the night with me."

She nodded and stepped between his spread legs. The sheet no longer covered the lower half of his body, and she realized that he slept in the nude. "You need only ask. I am yours, always."

He shook his head again. "I wish I could believe that. But for now this will be enough."

Abigail gave herself over to the moment. Words would never convince him, but perhaps with time her actions would show him that there could never be another man for her.

Cranston rested his head on her breast, his arms around her waist keeping her close. She continued to smooth her fingers through his hair, giving him the time he needed for the nightmare to pass. Warmth spread through her, and she willed him to take comfort from her presence.

As the minutes passed, heated longing started to grow within her. Along with the desire to do something for this man that they hadn't shared yet.

She slipped to her knees between his legs, her hands moving to his thighs. Before her eyes, his manhood, which was already half hard, began to stiffen and rise.

He cupped her chin and tilted her face up to him. "You don't have to…"

His words said one thing, but the desire in his eyes told her that he didn't want her to stop.

"I know. But I want to do this."

Her hands moved up his hard thighs, and she paused just before reaching his manhood, teasing out the moment. She brought her thumbs to the sides of his cock, touching him ever so lightly.

His leg muscles tensed under her arms, and she sensed he was holding back. She didn't know if it was because he feared hurting her with the strength of his need or if he thought that he needed to hold back because she was a gently bred young woman. But in that moment she wanted to see him lose control.

She reached down to cup the soft flesh of his sac, rolling his testicles gently in her hand. His breath hitched and then he let it out again in a hiss when she took him into her mouth.

"Abigail," he said on a moan, and the sound of his hoarse voice spurred her on.

Having never done this before, she knew her movements were awkward. His hands were now threaded in her hair, and when he moved her head back, she thought he was going to push her away from him.

Instead, he led her into a rhythm, her mouth on him mimicking the act of their lovemaking.

"Suck me," he said.

She obeyed, and his groan told her that she was

doing this right. She was giving him pleasure instead of being the one to receive it at his hands, and the thought made her feel heady.

She couldn't take all of him into her mouth, and so she moved her hands to wrap them around the base of him as she continued to move up and down his length. Her jaw was starting to ache from the unfamiliar act, but she didn't care. She would do this all night if it would soothe him. It was enough just to be with him like this.

He let out another long moan, and she knew he was close. She had a moment of wondering what would happen now. Would she swallow down his seed? Did it make her a wanton that she very much wanted to do that?

She'd started to speed up, looking forward to the moment he would explode in her mouth, when he pushed her away from him.

She made a soft sound of protest and tried to move back, but he tilted her head up to him.

"You are the most beautiful woman I have ever known. But right now I need to be inside you."

She slid her hand up and down his length, loving the way he clenched his teeth at her touch. Oh yes, he'd been close to finishing in her mouth.

She stood and her hands went to the belt of her

dressing gown. Her eyes remained fixed on him as she loosened the belt and allowed the dressing gown to fall to the floor.

His eyes widened. "What on earth are you wearing?"

The way his eyes, then his large hands, roved along the red satin, had liquid heat flowing through her veins. He cupped her breasts, squeezing them, and then allowed his hands to slide along the fabric, dipping into all the cutouts along the way. Abigail had almost thrown this garment away, sure she'd never have the confidence to wear it for him, but now she was glad she hadn't.

He swore and lifted her up over his lap, her knees on either side of him. Without hesitation, she lowered herself onto his hard length with a soft mewl of contentment. Somehow it seemed more wicked that he was nude while she wore the barely there nightdress.

Apparently he was done allowing her to be in control of their lovemaking, because he rolled them over until he was on top of her. And then he began to make love to her, his hips thrusting into her harder than he'd ever taken her before.

She was so aroused that it didn't take her long

to reach her peak, panting his name in a prayer. He followed, thrusting deep and filling her.

She loved the way his weight pressed her down into the mattress, and they stayed like that for almost a full minute. Finally he pulled out of her.

He'd asked her to spend the night with him, but she was almost afraid to hope he'd meant those words literally. Now that they'd both reached completion, she held her breath, waiting to see if he would ask her to leave. She wasn't about to do so on her own accord.

Instead, he reached for the bedsheet and pulled it over them. He draped his arm over her and pulled her tightly to his chest, where she rested her cheek.

"Gideon?"

"Yes." His low voice rumbled against her cheek.

"Why didn't you come to me tonight?"

There was a long pause, and she thought he wasn't going to answer her question.

She was on the verge of falling asleep when he finally spoke. "Because you are dangerous to my sensibilities."

# CHAPTER 21

Abigail treasured the memory of that night, sleeping wrapped in her husband's arms. It didn't happen again, but Cranston was no longer avoiding her. In fact, he was visiting her bed every night before returning to his own chamber.

He didn't have another nightmare, so she had no excuse to visit him, much as she wanted to.

As the time approached for her monthly courses, she began to wonder if she could be with child. They had conceived Gemma after being together only once, but Abigail was older now. She'd learned that sometimes it took a while for conception to take place.

Still, she hoped that given their recent nightly lovemaking, she'd soon become pregnant. She would know within the day. Her courses were never late, and they were due to arrive tomorrow. She had to be patient until then, although her intuition was telling her that she would soon have good news for her husband.

They'd reached a settled place in their relationship. She wanted to give him another child so much she ached from the desire. Wanted to give him the opportunity to be with his child from birth. But she needed to wait until the time for her bleeding had passed so she wouldn't get his hopes up only to dash them later.

She ignored the headache that had been plaguing her all day and headed downstairs to join Cranston and Gemma for dinner, as was their nightly ritual. But throughout the meal, her thoughts kept returning to the hope that they would soon be a family of four.

She was imagining how she would share the news when her daughter's voice broke into her thoughts.

"Mama?"

Abigail looked at Gemma. "Yes?"

"Can we go?"

Abigail looked to Cranston, who was watching her closely, then back at Gemma. "I'm afraid I was woolgathering. Can you repeat your question?"

"Miss Phillips was reading a story that took place in Africa. It had monkeys."

"And I told her that we should go to the Tower and visit the royal menagerie there to see the monkeys."

Abigail tried to smile at the two loves of her life, but her headache was so much worse than it had been this morning.

"Are you unwell?" Cranston asked, his eyes narrowing on her.

She nodded. "I'll be fine. It's just a headache."

"You had a headache yesterday," Gemma said.

"And one the day before that," Cranston added.

She lifted a hand to her temple. "It's not the first time I've had several so close together. I'm sure I'll be better soon."

Cranston didn't look convinced, but when he looked at Gemma and saw the way her brows were lowered with concern, he did what he could to set their daughter's mind at ease.

"We'll arrange for that visit as soon as your mother is feeling well." He turned to her. "Perhaps you should go upstairs and get some rest."

She nodded once, the pounding in her head

suddenly worse. "I think that's a good idea." When Cranston looked as though he was about to stand, she placed a hand on his arm. "You and Gemma should enjoy dessert. I know that Cook has prepared a syllabub."

His eyes roamed over her face. "Fine. But I will check on you later when I see Gemma to bed."

She stood, ignoring the way her vision swam for a moment. She leaned down to place a kiss on top of Gemma's head and said her good-nights.

She'd only just started to climb the stairs when the moment of dizziness came crashing back with a vengeance. She cried out as she crumpled. Her last action before losing consciousness was to send up a prayer for the child that she was now convinced she carried.

"Is Mama going to get well?" Gemma asked. "Maybe I should bring Pepper for a visit."

"I'm sure she will. But I think she needs to rest for a little while before she can play with the kitten." He was trying to convince himself as much as his daughter, but in truth he was more than a little concerned. Three days of headaches seemed excessive. And she'd been getting paler with each passing day. If she wasn't better tomorrow, he'd send for a physician.

When he heard her cry out, he leapt to his feet. The chair made a horrible scraping sound as he pushed it back and raced to see what had happened.

He found Abigail slumped at the bottom of the stairs, her head on the second stair.

His heart was already racing as he hurried to her side. How far had she fallen? Had she hit her head on the way down?

Servants were starting to crowd into the hallway.

He crouched, his years of military service kicking into action as he looked her over. He didn't see any blood. After ensuring she was still breathing, he looked at the side of her head. There wasn't any blood, but a small bump was beginning to form at her temple.

He didn't realize that Gemma had followed him into the hallway until he heard her gasp.

"Mama!" Tears began to flow down her face.

"Fetch a doctor," he commanded the nearest footman. Then he turned to his daughter. It was a struggle to keep his voice even. "Gemma, your mother is going to need you to be strong for her. Do you think you can do that?"

She nodded. The tears didn't stop, but they did slow.

"Good girl. I'm going to make sure she's okay and then carry her to her bed."

"Can I stay with you?"

"Of course," he said. "But we need to be strong so we can take care of her."

She nodded. "I can do that."

He turned back to his wife and started to look her over. Carefully he examined her arms and then her legs to see if she had any broken bones. He let out a breath when he didn't detect any breaks.

He'd seen his fair share of injuries on the battle-field, and this was a task he'd hoped never to perform again.

He ran his hands over her body, carefully watching her face for even the smallest grimace of pain. He held his breath as he ran a hand along her spine, then along her ribs. Finally he probed gently at her neck. He'd seen men with broken necks before, and it almost made him physically ill to consider that his wife could be hurt in a similar manner.

When he detected no sign of injury aside from

the small lump at her temple, he shifted her body with care and then lifted her into his arms.

He moved more slowly than normal, trying to keep his pace even as he carried her upstairs and down the hall. He didn't have to ask Gemma to open Abigail's bedchamber door, and then he was placing her on the bed with care.

When he stood by the bedside, a hollow ache in his chest as he stared down at Abigail, Gemma slipped her hand into his. Gemma's breathing was uneven, but his daughter had done an admirable job of calming her tears.

"I'm scared," she said.

Heaven help him, so was he. But he wouldn't give voice to the words. Nothing bad would happen to Abigail.

He couldn't lose her again.

He wasn't shocked by his realization that he was still in love with this woman. That he would gladly trade places with her right now if it meant she would be well.

His feelings had been there for some time now, simmering just below his consciousness. He'd refused to think about them, dwelling instead on the fact that the two of them were companionable and that he was content with their marriage in its current state.

*Companionable.*

He wanted to laugh at his own stupidity. For trying to convince himself that he could live with Abigail, make love to her, and keep his emotions locked away.

He'd wanted to protect himself, but in the end he'd failed to do that. The only thing he'd succeeded in doing was making her unhappy.

Oh, she tried to hide it, but he could see the hurt in her eyes whenever he turned away from her. Hell, he'd seen it when he told her outright that he could never love her again.

Now he needed her to live so that he could tell her he'd been a fool. So that he could beg her forgiveness and ask her if she could ever come to love him again.

There was a soft knock at the door, and then it swung open and an older man stepped into the room.

"I'm Dr. Harris," he said, his eyes already roving over Abigail. "Tell me exactly what happened."

Consciousness came back to Abigail slowly. Wondering what time it was, she opened her eyes and turned toward the window. The drapes were open and it was still dark out. Relief flooded through her when she realized that her headache was almost gone. She raised a hand to her temple and found there was something on it. A bandage?

Then she remembered her fainting spell while on the stairs. Someone must have brought her to her room.

She turned to look at the small clock she kept on her bedside table and was surprised to see Cranston slumped in an armchair that had been moved into the room. Dark stubble lined his jaw.

Had he been worried about her fall?

Ice-cold dread settled in her belly as she remembered her final thought before fainting. With a soft sob, her hand went to her midsection. She didn't need to wait until she'd missed her monthly courses to know she was with child. Fainting spells had plagued her only one other time in her life—when she was carrying Gemma.

How far had she fallen? Clearly she'd injured her head, but had she also risked her pregnancy? It was still early, and she knew that falls could cause a woman to miscarry.

She shifted into a seated position on the bed. "Gideon?"

His eyes snapped open. He rose from the armchair and moved to sit on the edge of her bed.

"Did I faint?" she asked, knowing the question was a foolish one.

He nodded.

"I apologize for worrying you." Her hand rose to her temple. "Did you do this? Did I bang my head on the stairs?"

She wanted to ask if she'd bled elsewhere but was afraid to hear the answer.

He grasped one of her hands. The intensity of his stare frightened her, and she feared the worst.

"What is the matter? Why are you looking at me like that?"

"Abigail, you fainted on the stairs two days ago. I called for a doctor immediately and he bandaged your temple. I…" He closed his eyes, and a spasm of pain crossed his face. "We didn't know how far you'd fallen. I was so afraid you'd hurt yourself… And then when you didn't wake up…"

She gripped his hand between both of hers. "I'd only taken two stairs when I felt weakness overtake me."

His eyes scoured her face, and then he dragged her into his arms.

"Never scare me like that again." He spoke into her hair, his breath warm against her scalp, before dropping a kiss onto her head.

"I'm sorry for worrying you," she said. "Oh no—what did you tell Gemma when I didn't come down for breakfast yesterday?"

He pulled back to look down at her as though she'd lost her mind. "We heard you call out after leaving the dining room. Gemma was at my side when I found you. She's been worried sick. She's been spending her days here, drawing pictures for you and reading to you."

Her hand went to her mouth, and she choked

back a sob. "Oh, my poor baby. I must go to her now."

She started to get out of bed, but he held her in place. "I checked on her before coming in here to watch over you. She's sound asleep."

"But—"

"As you told me, Miss Phillips has the bedchamber next to hers. If Gemma wakes up frightened, her governess will hear her. And she has instructions to contact me no matter what time it is."

Abigail took a deep breath, trying to calm her concern. "I hate that she's had to see me like this."

"Our daughter is a wonder. You've done an amazing job with her. She was frightened when she first saw you, but she pulled herself together quickly and showed a strength of spirit that amazed me."

Abigail let out a sigh. "She's always reminded me of you. The way everyone loves her, how her spirit refuses to be daunted."

Cranston shook his head. "Abigail, you've just described yourself."

She made a soft scoffing sound. "I recall you not liking me very much, and that wasn't very long ago. I imagine you spent years hating me."

One corner of his mouth lifted. "Perhaps, but I

was a fool in love who'd been thwarted. My feelings about you after that fact weren't exactly reasonable."

She looked away at his reminder that his love for her was firmly in the past.

"Why didn't you tell me you were with child?"

Her gaze swung to his. "What?"

"Dr. Harris told me that it is his belief that you're with child. Fainting and headaches can be a symptom in the early days."

Her hand went to her abdomen. "I didn't know about the headaches. As for the other... I didn't want to say anything until I was certain. I hadn't yet missed my courses."

"But you knew about the fainting."

She nodded. "It happened when I was carrying Gemma. But this was the first time I've fainted since then." She bit her lip, afraid to ask the next question.

He took hold of the hand that was covering her belly and held it in his. "You look concerned."

"My fall... It's possible that I could have..." Her voice hitched, and she had to start again. "I might have lost the baby."

He brought her hand to his mouth and dropped

a kiss in her palm. "Your maid has been checking, and there's been no sign of any blood."

She couldn't hold back her smile. "That means… I'm carrying our child."

His mouth widened in a pleased smile. "So it would seem. But it appears I'll have to assign someone to accompany you up and down the stairs."

She shook her head at his teasing tone. "Normally I'd be annoyed at your overbearing tone, but I, too, don't want to take any risks with the life of our child."

He cupped her cheek with his other hand. "Or with your life, Abigail."

Her breath caught. "Well no, of course not. I promise to be careful until the baby is born."

He shook his head. "You misunderstand me. When I saw you slumped at the bottom of the stairs…" His expression turned grim. "I can't lose you again, Abigail."

She couldn't be hearing him correctly. She stared into his eyes and saw the same haunted look she'd seen when she'd woken him from his nightmare.

"What are you saying, Gideon?"

He ran his thumb along her lower lip. "I'm

saying that apparently I'm still a fool because I've never stopped loving you."

Her heart was pounding. "Don't tease about that. I don't need you to pretend—"

Her words were cut off by a searing kiss that left her breathless. Finally, when he'd rendered her speechless, he pulled back and stared down at her. "I would never lie about such a thing. I love you, Abigail."

She let out a soft sob and flung her arms around his shoulders. His arms went around her as he held her tightly against his chest.

"I've never stopped loving you. But I couldn't allow myself to believe…" She drew back, a sense of giddy wonder overtaking her. The last time she'd felt this way was when Cranston had professed his love for her all those years ago and asked her to marry him.

He cupped her face in his hands and kissed her again. "I think we have some time to make up for."

"No more keeping me at arm's length?"

One corner of his mouth kicked up in a wicked grin. "Absolutely not. From now on, you'll be remaining firmly in my arms."

"That's the only place I want to be."

# EPILOGUE

*February 1818*

Abigail made her way to her husband's study half an hour before Gemma would be joining them for dinner. As she slid into the room, she took a moment to watch her husband. She still couldn't believe that the man who was currently scribbling away, his brow furrowed in concentration, was now an important part of her life.

She cleared her throat, and Cranston let out a distracted "Just one moment" as he continued to make notes. Finally he put down his quill and glanced up.

"Abigail. I thought you were one of the staff." He jumped to his feet and led her to one of the two armchairs set in a corner of the study. "You shouldn't be on your feet."

She laughed. "I was on my feet for two minutes."

He dropped into a crouch before her and placed a hand on her belly. She still had three months before their baby was due to arrive but of late was already finding it difficult to sit and to stand again. She feared how big she'd be if the baby inside her continued to grow at this alarming rate.

Cranston moved to the second armchair. He leaned forward and took hold of her hand. "I'm not going to apologize for wanting you to be safe."

She shook her head in amusement, unable to believe just how much Cranston had changed in the short time they'd been wed.

"I saw your brother today in Parliament. He'll be joining us for dinner tonight."

"Oh, that's good news indeed," she said. "I've scarce seen him the past two weeks since he arrived in town."

Cranston shrugged. "He's been busy settling matters with your father's town house and with the solicitors. He'll probably be busy for some time yet as he grows into his role as the new Earl of Hargrove. Still, I managed to apply enough guilt about how you're desperate to see him."

Abigail tried to scowl at him, but they both knew he was speaking the truth. "I should tell the butler to let him in the moment he arrives…"

She started to rise, but Cranston shook his head. "There's no need. I've already told the staff that your brother is welcome here at any time."

Another warmth of affection flowed through her. She knew the pregnancy was making her more emotional, but she loved how Cranston had been so welcoming to her one remaining family member. The only one, really, who'd ever supported her.

There was a soft knock at the door. At Cranston's command, the door opened and, almost as if they'd summoned him with their words, Geoffrey stepped into the room.

He shook his head as he stared at their joined hands. "Father would be rolling over in his grave if he could see the two of you now."

"Geoff!" Abigail rose to her feet more slowly than she would have liked and wrapped her arms around her brother.

"Hargrove," Cranston said by way of greeting as he stood.

Her brother winced. "I don't think I'll ever get used to that. Especially since the mere thought of the former earl is enough to set my blood boiling today."

"Oh no." Abigail threaded her arm through her brother's and guided him out into the hallway and to the drawing room where they could all be seated comfortably. "Perhaps I shouldn't have abandoned you when I did to come to London."

When she released her brother's arm, Cranston helped her onto the settee and settled next to her. "Well, I for one am glad you came to town when you did."

Geoffrey collapsed into an armchair, his legs and arms sprawled. "The two of you are nauseating."

Abigail smiled fondly at her husband before turning to examine her brother. She couldn't help but feel a twinge of guilt. Their father would have been very angry when she escaped his attempts to force her into another marriage of his choosing. "It's been over a month since he passed. You can do whatever you wish now without his interference."

Her brother snorted. "I received a letter this morning from Lord Appleby. My betrothed's father."

She couldn't have heard him correctly. "I didn't know you were courting."

"Neither did I. Father arranged it when I was young and didn't see fit to tell me about it until he was on his deathbed."

Cranston snorted. "Why am I not surprised?" He went to the sideboard and poured a drink, then returned and pressed it into her brother's hand.

With a nod of thanks, her brother tossed back the contents of the glass and set it on the side table.

Her husband returned to her side. "Have you looked into the matter? If it was merely a verbal agreement, it should be easy enough to have set aside. I might know someone who could advise you."

"I thought the old man was lying when he told me. He'd been trying to get me to court Lydia Pearce for some time now. He became particularly persistent toward the end when it became clear that he wasn't going to recover."

"If no formal agreement was made…" Abigail raised one shoulder. "Surely it would be no different than when I fled the house to avoid Father pressing a match between me and Lord Gravenhurst."

"Gravenhurst?" Her husband scowled. "You didn't tell me that."

She placed a soothing hand on his knee. "It was never going to happen. With the support I was receiving from my husband's heir, Father couldn't force me to marry again." And especially not to another older man who liked to marry young women. Gravenhurst had already gone through two wives. No doubt he was considering Abigail only because she'd proven that she wouldn't die during childbirth.

Geoffrey let out a mirthless laugh. "I saw the family solicitor this afternoon, and a formal agreement does exist."

Abigail's heart fell. "There must be some way out of it."

"According to the terms of the contract, both parties must be in agreement for the betrothal to be broken. And according to the letter I received today, Miss Pearson is quite anxious to marry me. They'll be arriving in London within the week."

Abigail met her husband's concerned gaze before looking at her brother again. "Maybe the two of you will get on well. Or conversely, she'll be just as opposed to the betrothal and you can set aside the agreement."

"Unless her parents are forcing the match and she has no choice in the matter," Cranston said.

Her brother glared at him. "Such a ray of sunshine. I can see why you married him, Abby."

The sound of hurried footsteps announced Gemma's arrival long before she rushed into the room.

"Uncle Geoffrey," she exclaimed before launching herself into his arms.

Her brother stood and twirled Gemma around in a circle, much to her daughter's delight.

"Well, that's enough about glum subjects." He put Gemma on the floor and took hold of her hand. "Your father told me you have a cat now. Would you like to introduce us before dinner?"

Gemma turned pleading eyes on her and Cranston. "Can I?"

Abigail smiled. "Of course. But dinner will be served soon, so you'll have to be quick."

She watched them leave, Gemma telling her uncle how Pepper had gotten into the kitchen today and tried to sample the beef that Cook was preparing for their dinner.

Abigail turned to Cranston. "Perhaps things will work out."

Cranston lifted a brow. "Have you met Viscount Appleby and his wife? Or their daughter for that matter?"

The tone in his voice wasn't promising. "No, but—"

"Your brother will have his work cut out for him trying to get out of this marriage. And I have no doubt he'll want to."

She leaned against him, and he placed his arm around her shoulders. "I hope Father hasn't doomed both his children to unhappy marriages. At least my husband was older and the marriage of relatively short duration."

He dropped a quick kiss onto her lips. "We'll see what we can do to help him."

Thank you for reading *The Baron's Return!* I hope you enjoyed reading Abigail and Cranston's story. If you want more, there is a bonus epilogue available! Sign up for my newsletter at https://www.suzannamedeiros.com/newsletter to get access to my bonus content!

The Earl of Hargrove's (Geoffrey's) story is next in *Courting the Earl.*

Turn the page for an excerpt from A Viscount for Christmas, which is book 1 in my CHRISTMAS SCANDALS series.

# EXCERPT—A VISCOUNT FOR CHRISTMAS

*An unexpected Christmas gift…*

When Viscount Isaac Thornton returns home for his mother's annual Christmas gathering, the last thing he expects to find is a beautiful woman sleeping in his bed. But Celia isn't yet another woman trying to trap him into marriage. She's his younger sister's best friend and now she's all grown up.

Celia Rowland outgrew the infatuation she had for Thornton years ago. When a misunderstanding means she's been compromised, her mother insists they get married.

One house party and two people trying to escape a forced wedding who just might get the Christmas gift they didn't know they wanted.

*December 1816*

It was past midnight when Viscount Isaac Thornton reached his estate in Surrey. He'd been on horseback for several hours. Normally the ride wasn't a difficult one, but with the cold temperatures, he'd needed to stop frequently to change horses.

Filled with a bone-deep fatigue that emphasized the unwelcome fact he'd recently passed his thirtieth birthday, all he wanted to do was sleep. He wasn't looking forward to the next week. His mother's yearly Christmas party would be yet another opportunity for her to remind him he needed to settle down and produce an heir. He couldn't avoid his mother's matchmaking altogether, but he could limit the duration of his suffering. Which was why he'd originally planned to arrive the day before Christmas and depart again the day after the holiday.

She'd successfully thwarted those plans with the greatest weapon in her arsenal—guilt. He'd received her letter that afternoon. In it, she told him how much she looked forward to spending quality time with him. She'd gone on to inform him that his two younger sisters, who lived in the north of England, wouldn't be attending because the roads were impassable after a heavy snowfall that hadn't reached Surrey. To alleviate what he knew would be her very real disappointment, he'd changed his plans and set out to join her when her house party would still be in full swing.

If he were being honest with himself, London had become tedious of late, especially after his friends and most of his acquaintances quit town and headed to their own estates for the holiday season. His mother's letter was a convenient excuse to return home earlier than planned.

He apologized to the sleepy groom who greeted him moments after he reached the stables. He was relieved to discover the manor was quiet as he made his way to the front door on foot. Perhaps his mother hadn't invited that many people this year.

But even as the thought occurred to him, he knew it was a futile wish. Christmas was his mother's favorite time of the year, and she was known for her winter house parties. This year wouldn't be any different.

He was surprised when the front door was opened by Saunders, their butler, and not a footman. He'd hoped to surprise his mother, but apparently she knew him too well. She'd expected him to set out for Surrey after receiving her letter.

He greeted the older man and handed him his hat and greatcoat, barely taking in the evergreen boughs and festive decorations that tastefully highlighted the fact the festive season was upon them. He'd started toward the stairs when Saunders coughed discreetly.

Thornton turned to face him.

"Your mother wishes to speak with you, my lord."

Thornton frowned. No doubt she wanted to tell him who she'd invited and why he should pay particular attention to each one of them. He'd just arrived, and already the matchmaking had begun.

He nodded. "I'll speak to her in the morning."

"She insisted—"

Thornton wouldn't take his annoyance out on this man whom he'd known since he was a child. Saunders was merely carrying out Lady Thornton's instructions.

"I already know what she wants to speak to me about."

"But—"

"Good night, Saunders. I'll speak to my mother first thing in the morning. And get some rest yourself." The man had no doubt been awake since dawn.

Before Saunders could say another word, Thornton turned and made his way upstairs.

He didn't ring for his valet when he reached his bedroom, too tired to care about the lecture the man would deliver tomorrow as he tossed his clothes onto a chair.

*-It was dark, but he didn't need to light a candle. He made his way to the bed and slid under the covers. His eyes were closing when a small movement on the other side of the bed chased away his fatigue.

He was imagining things. Or, more likely, he'd already fallen asleep and was dreaming. Still, he was wide awake now. He rolled over and narrowed his gaze on the other side of the bed, where he could see a small bundle wrapped in his blankets.

In retrospect, he should have sprung from the bed and thrown on his clothes. But he didn't really expect to find anything, and so he pulled back the bedsheets. It took his befuddled senses several seconds to process the fact he wasn't alone.

Someone was already asleep in his bed—a woman, to be precise. She lay with her back to him, and he could only stare at her for what felt like the longest minute of his life.

His fumbling in the dark hadn't caused her to move, so she must be asleep. His gaze took in the long golden hair that covered most of her back. Unbound, which surprised him. Unable to stop himself, he gazed down to where her hair ended just above the curve of her hip, which was covered in a white nightgown. The blankets covered the rest of her, and he resisted the temptation to drag them down even farther.

Casting aside the temptation to see whether she would be well endowed, he shifted onto his back and slung a hand over his eyes. He doubted very much that his mother had arranged this woman as a welcome-home present for him. She'd probably wanted to warn him that she had given away his room to another guest.

Which meant he had to dress again and find a servant to lead him to a room that was unoccupied.

He rose to a seating position with a muffled groan. He thought he'd been quiet, but the shifting of his weight must have woken the woman, because she rolled onto her back. Her eyes blinked open, and she let out a sleepy yawn. And then a scream.

That should have had him moving with alacrity, gathering up his clothes and escaping into the dressing room. But his brief glimpse at her form before she'd pulled up the bedcovers caused him to freeze. In the dim light, he could see that she was, indeed, well endowed.

Why did these things never happen to him under better circumstances? For it was clear now that he wasn't dreaming. If he were, she would have beckoned him to her with open arms. Instead, the woman in his bed had gathered up the blankets and held them to her breast like a shield.

"What are you doing here? You must leave at once!"

Yes, this wasn't a dream. "This is my bedroom."

Her mouth gaped open before she closed it with a snap. "You're not suggesting…" She took a deep breath and began again. "We can sort out this mess tomorrow morning. But a gentleman would leave without question and find another bedroom."

He couldn't resist teasing her. "Perhaps I'm not a gentleman."

She sputtered, speechless. Taking pity on her, he slipped from the bed with a soft curse.

"I don't know why you're upset. I'm the injured party here."

Something about the prim tone of her voice seemed familiar. He strode to the window and drew back the curtains to let in some of the moonlight. Then he returned to the bed—the side the woman occupied—and leaned forward to examine her. She leaned back with a squawk.

His eyes roamed over her face. Blond hair, blue eyes… she could have been anyone. But then he saw the small mole at the corner of her right eye.

"Celia Rowland?"

She huffed out an impatient breath. "That's Miss Rowland to you, my lord. Now will you please leave?"

He had to give her credit. Another woman might have given in to a fit of vapors at finding a man in her bed, but not Celia. He remembered her only as his youngest sister's friend. She'd been pretty, and he remembered finding her sweet, but she'd also been much too young for him the last time he'd seen her. He couldn't deny that she'd grown into a beautiful young woman.

He didn't miss the way her gaze dipped to his

bare chest and couldn't hold back his smirk. "Like what you see?"

Her eyes met his again. "I was merely—"

"Admiring my fine form? Wondering if you'd asked me to leave too soon?"

She let out an impatient huff. "Is it your intention to compromise me?"

And that's when the reality of the situation settled into place. His understanding came too late, however, because the bedroom door was thrown open.

# BOOKS BY SUZANNA MEDEIROS

Dear Stranger

Forbidden in February (A Year Without a Duke multi-author series)

**Anthologies:**

The Novellas: A Collection

Hathaway Heirs: Books 1-4

Landing a Lord: Books 1-3

**Landing a Lord series:**

Dancing with the Duke

Loving the Marquess

Beguiling the Earl

The Unaffected Earl

The Unsuitable Duke

The Unexpected Marquess

The Unwilling Viscount

The Baron's Return

Courting the Earl (Coming next!)

**Christmas Scandals series:**

A Viscount for Christmas

A Highwayman for Christmas

**Hathaway Heirs series:**

Lady Hathaway's Proposal

Lord Hathaway's Bride

Captain Hathaway's Dilemma

Miss Hathaway's Wish

For more information please visit the author's website:
https://www.suzannamedeiros.com/books/

USA Today bestselling author Suzanna Medeiros was born and raised in Toronto, Canada. Her love for the written word led her to pursue a degree in English Literature from the University of Toronto. She went on to earn a Bachelor of Education degree but graduated at a time when no teaching jobs were available. After working at a number of interesting places, including a federal inquiry, a youth probation office, and the Office of the Fire Marshal of Ontario, she decided to pursue her first love—writing.

Suzanna is married to her own hero and is the proud mother of twin daughters. She is an avowed romantic who enjoys spending her days writing love stories.

She would like to thank her parents for showing her that love at first sight and happily ever after really do exist.

To learn about Suzanna Medeiros's future books (and to receive a bonus short story!) sign up for her newsletter:
https://www.suzannamedeiros.com/newsletter

Visit her website:
https://www.suzannamedeiros.com

Or visit her on Facebook:
https://www.facebook.com/
AuthorSuzannaMedeiros

www.ingramcontent.com/pod-product-compliance
Lightning Source LLC
Chambersburg PA
CBHW032028310726
48972CB00002B/574